BETWEEN THE LINES

SHIRLEY DAY

PUBLISHED WITH
PASSION

Created with Vellum

To Julia Shepherd, my library manager, who had a smile, a joke, a book and a kind word for everyone.
A true star.

"Our crime section inhabits three carousels. Not to mention Large Crime, large print that is, not large as in high body count. But, of course, there are different types of murder. Most people don't want graphic detail. They want a nice, tidy, comfortable murder, clean and aesthetic in a rural setting, with lots of motive. Which is exactly what we had."

— JULIA. LIBRARY MANAGER.

1

FITNESS

If the weather were kind, Julia would ride her bike the long way to work. It was an odd decision. Julia was no spring chicken and to call the road circuitous would be a kindness it did not deserve. The route involved a long, zig-zag of a climb up Potter's Rise. The potholed winding road was far less inviting than the beloved Greenlane, which embraced the outskirts of the village in a satisfying ring. Yet Julia had always favoured the more circuitous route, partly, perhaps, because it flanked the eastern boundary of Hortishall Hall, an Elizabethan baroque masterpiece. Sadly, the Hall was no longer visible from the road since the (misguided—many said) planting of a leylandii hedge in the mid-1990s. The leylandii hedge would be enough to put most people off taking the road with its ugly, great strapping trees. Gargantuan structures left the darkened road smelling eerily of lemon and pine—an unlikely combination for rural Suffolk. It was unclear who had thought the hedge would be a good idea. Curtis Crabapple had been a gardener at the Hall since he was a lad yet had not been consulted.

Suffice it to say, when Lord and Lady Hortishall had put the hedge in all those years ago, a bitter disappointment had fallen over the village; the community had realised—in what could only be described as a wave of resounding grief—that they were powerless to protect the places they loved. Places such as Hortishall Hall which seemed somehow entwined with their very being—most of the villagers having been born, raised and heading graveside, within the confines of the village.

The hedge should never have been brought up at the council meetings. Although an eye-sore, it did not directly affect the villagers and could not be seen through anyone's windows. Yet up it came as certain as the contents of a hotdog stand after the local fair has wheeled its weary way out of town. It was the Historical Association who had brought the matter to the table. They said that the hedge was not in keeping. Another problem with such hedges, they had pointed out, was the attraction and proliferation of unwanted accompaniments such as jimson weed—a trumpet-shaped climber with a toxic habit and passion for invading the gardens of others. Sadly, the Historical Association had been buoyed up since the council's successful removal of Mark Tanner's hedge. As everyone who has lived past the age of forty knows all too well—success can be a danger. It has the potential to swell the brain as surely as encephalitis.

Like Julia, Mark was a newcomer to the area and had planted his leylandii as soon as he had moved into his cottage. A naturist by heart, Mark had explained to his neighbour Lillian Kemp that it was either see him naked or enjoy the spread of his trees. After ten years of darkness, poor Lillian was diagnosed with SAD—Seasonal Affective Disorder. She said she would opt for the light and the full-frontal. When the trees came down, the entire community breathed a sigh of relief, and luckily, since Mark was well into his eighties by that time, he no longer fancied airing himself in quite the same way he had done in his younger years. It was a situation avoided. A battle won peacefully.

But winning battles with the landed gentry might not be so easily done, something the village council were all too aware of. People had been murdered over leylandii, a fact Julia had discovered when she had been asked to look into the history of hedging and report back. The job of a rural library manager may be many things, but it is never dull. Julia was also aware that His Lordship kept fencing foils over his mantelpiece, and there was a cannon on the lawn.

Julia's findings sent up warning flags. The village knew they were powerless against the owners of the Hall. Just because you've been lucky on the gargantuan conifer front once does not mean that your luck will last. If no one took the road past the Hall, the leylandii could triffid themselves into eternity with not one person being any the wiser, more shaded, or more upset. Everyone used the main entrance of the estate for the annual summer fair back then anyway, so nobody would be forced into an unfortunate hedging encounter.

Yet cycling past the Hall's eastern border seemed to be a bit of a tradition for Julia. If asked, and let's face it, people did ask, it was that kind of a village - nothing went unnoticed, - so, in amendment, *when asked*, she would reply that the ride was good for her thighs and buttocks. This normally shuts the conversation down pretty quickly. Julia was a big woman in many ways, and well respected. Understandably, people did not want to go thinking about Julia's thighs and buttocks. So, thankfully, she had been released to cycle the lanes on her own: past the Hall, smiling at the bird song, marvelling at the leylandii, and enjoying God's green pastures before arriving at work and having to tackle the library burglar alarm, which was always a point of stress.

Even in a small village, library life can be taxing. Although it was true, that they had never had a break-in or a theft, there was still the overdue to deal with, the unwanted and the damaged, and all of that was without even picking up a book. People can be odd in the country.

When his Lordship passed suddenly after his heart stopped, it was also noted that Julia appeared to have a slight flush to her cheeks. Was this down to the possibility that the hedge might also be on its way out? Or perhaps more likely, it could be due to the exercise. It had been noted that Julia had started cycling her route twice a day since the old guy had gone. She was reported as saying that she liked the 'quiet' 'the thinking time,' and 'the peace.'

Only this morning - twenty years after the concerns over the hedge, and barely eighteen months after his Lordship had "left," the normally oh-so-quiet flat strip of tarmac echoed not with bird song but with sirens. Police Vehicles drove in a line like a spray of caterpillars on speed. Their neon lights flared, bouncing cruelly off the green wall of leylandii as they nearly knocked poor Julia out of their path.

She stopped, pushing her toes into the soft, springy September earth so that her bike was fully supported. She watched curiously as the cars trailed past in their long, steady procession—four of them. Now as everybody knows, one car could be for delivering news or investigating a natural tragedy. They had sent one car when Lord Hortishall snored his last. Two, there might have been an attempted burglary; there would certainly be things within the house worth taking. Three vehicles, could be for tax evasion, but four? Julia knew all too well that police cars had their semaphoric system just as sure as magpies and that four cars had to mean something far more sinister than a heart-stopping or a few candlesticks being re-appropriated from a marble mantlepiece. Four cars surely had to mean murder.

2

IT STARTED

Eighteen Months Earlier, one fine but cold January morning, as Julia had been enjoying the peace and quiet of her cycle, she heard the slow tread of tyres behind and felt her heart sink. Had Carris, Julia's flaky but loyal library assistant, attempted to open up on her own? Had the alarm gone off? With a resigned sigh, Julia pulled her bike to the side, twisting her body to see who could be following her on this cold winter morning. What she saw struck her as odd. Out of place. For there behind her was the police—one car with no lights or sirens. She smiled at PC Mumblings, the sole occupant of the vehicle, as it crawled slowly past. PC Gary Mumblings was biting his large lip as though apprehensive. It was unusual for Gary on two accounts, he barely strayed out of the village, and also, he didn't do "apprehensive". Gary was, in fact, habitually and, often unfortunately, an overconfident man. He barely noticed Julia pulled up beside the verge, didn't even wave at her, which was also odd because Julia had known Gary since he was a lad. In his younger years, he had acquired the unfortunate habit of sticking chewing gum under a computer station, and although the practice had stopped promptly enough, to Julia's mind, Gary had never been fully accounted for his crime. As always with parents and misdemeanours, it was Mrs Mumblings who had eventually delivered some kind of sad ventriloquist-style apology before making young Gary clean away the rock-hard creation he'd been constructing on the underside of the desk. But that was a long time ago, and who would have thought then that Gary Mumblings would be driving anything more than the red and yellow rocket scooter he'd terrorised the village from at the age of ten, let alone that he'd be driving a vehicle of authority.

Julia glanced at her watch as Gary clicked on his indicator and disappeared through the gap in the leylandii. This gap housed the eastern gateway to the great Hall—the tradesperson's approach.

Calendar-wise, it would have been opportune timing for a police visit. The Suffolk Coastal Constabulary might well want to wrangle a little funding out of the Hortishalls for the inevitable January police ball. It was a sore subject since this particular year, the entire force had fallen back on their favourite, sadly predictable, theme of saints and sinners. If they had asked Julia, with her considerable literary knowledge, she could have suggested a host of other themes. However, she had always maintained an attitude of quiet observance. If people didn't ask, she didn't tell. Although Julia tilted her head thoughtfully in a stream of bright early morning sunshine, a plea for funding did not fit the facts. It wasn't even eight-thirty. This visit was far too early for a social call.

Slowly, she glided her wheels towards the gate, barely pushing the bike's pedals and came to rest by one of the twin stone pillars framing this secondary, more modest,

Hortishall driveway. There she waited, gazed down upon as she stood by twin stone eagles that had landed there in the nineteenth century. She waited quietly with the granite birds for a good half hour before deciding the matter must be grave, as PC Mullings did not come back out. It appeared that all was not well at Hortishall Hall.

~

'LATE,' grumbled the damp pile of clothes from the library steps where it crouched. Not even a "hello". Geoff might have recently acquired himself a BA in independent film-making, but he was sadly lacking on the manners front.

Uncharacteristically, Julia didn't bother to reply. It had been a rush to get down the hill, and her mind was still puzzling over the mystery. Why would one police car be driving up to the Hall? Something didn't make sense.

She dismounted leisurely from her bike, removing the bicycle clips which held her viscose slacks firmly in place. She felt a bite of disappointment that Carris hadn't managed to unlock the building. Surely, it wasn't much to ask. In fact, it was in the handbook—a manager could be late on occasion, providing they didn't make a habit of it. The flow chart was unequivocal: "In the event of a manager's unforeseen tardiness, others should take on the relevant duties." But the dark, blank windows of the library and the fact that the swinging "Welcome All" notice board had not been parked on the steps, clanking in the early winter breeze, meant that Carris was sadly missing in action.

'Nice greeting, Geoff,' Julia huffed, still a little breathless from the fast peddle she'd had to adopt on the downward slope of Potter's Rise (commonly known as Potter's Descent). 'Pleasure to see you too.' The lad hung around the library so much, anyone would be forgiven for assuming he worked there. Only he didn't. "*Work*" and "*Geoff*" were two words never to be found in close company. Julia glided the front wheel of her bike effortlessly into the splayed metal jaws of the council-provided bike lock. 'Besides, Geoff, I've got things on my mind.' She said, fishing in the wide utility pockets of her coat for the keys.

'Grumph,' Geoff grunted, pulling himself awkwardly to his feet. For a young man, Geoff tended to do an awful lot of grunting. 'We've all got things on our minds.'

Julia doubted this was, in fact, true where Geoff was concerned, not that she didn't like the lad. Julia didn't believe in judging. This was one of her best qualities. Life was too short for public trial and irritation. Live and let live, that was Julia. Besides, she'd always found people do love to surprise you. 'No Carris?' she asked, pushing the key into the lock.

Geoff glanced back down the road, his dark, vacant eyes attempting to narrow in concentration. 'Thought I saw her look around the corner earlier, but maybe not. Whoever it was just disappeared off.'

Julia sighed. She had to do something about this. It wasn't just the handbook which stated Carris should have been on site holding the fort; the matter went deeper. Then again, none of that was Geoff's business. Although it was, in fact, a mystery as to what exactly Geoff's business was. Only one thing was for sure: it certainly had nothing to do with library management.

'Hands covering ears,' Julia shouted brightly over her shoulder in Geoff's direction. She pushed open the door as the sharp scream of the alarm filled the air, and Julia threw herself through the rattling library entrance, careful to avoid the dropped book pile— a spray of titles pushed hastily through the letterbox in a last-ditch attempt to avoid fines.

A copy of a celebrity biography slithered under Julia's foot as she passed quickly over the coarse coir entry mat. This part of the job was always tricky. There was no time for foot wiping. The alarm was getting louder, wailing like an embryonic banshee that was showing promise. Grabbing the broom, which she always stationed at the side of the door when she left for the evening, Julia extended its long arm out over the reception desk, angling the broom's blunt end with the precision of a Swiss watchmaker at the alarm's off settings, before giving the plastic casing a quick jab.

Silence. A wonderful sense of calm fell instantly. For a moment, Julia wallowed in it. Was there anything so truly delicious as tranquillity? Then, remembering herself - the library should be open by now - she flipped on the lights. Slim, narrow strips of plastic-encased glass buzzed into action. The lights were the old-fashioned type, fluorescent and unflattering to both those who entered the library and the poor, sad library building itself. As she approached her sixtieth year, Julia didn't worry too much about the fact that the light washed out her skin, giving it a curious tinge of purple luminosity. It did that for everyone. Fluorescents were egalitarian in their ignorance of aesthetics. No, what she minded was the effect the harsh lighting had on her beloved library. Some might have been sniffy about calling this community venue a library. She had been on courses for the library service, where, indeed, some librarians had not been kind. But a library it was—one large rectangular room inhabited with obscure islands of book carousels and every wall crammed high with shelves. There was a small IT section consisting of three terminals (happily devoid of gum sculpturing) and a series of giant bean bags in one corner, indicating the Children's Corner. At one point, this area had been bright and inviting for the under-fives, but now it only looked gaudy and over-tired. A primary blue and red jigsaw of a rug attempted to mark the section off, and a sandpit-style rectangular trough of cover-worn books left the idle visitor in no doubt as to who this area was for.

'Julia was late,' Geoff announced gleefully, interrupting her thoughts.

She turned to see Carris cowering slightly at the library entrance. The woman's small frame leaned hesitantly in the doorway, crumpled into apologetic angles. A look of apprehension stamped on her face.

'Fifteen minutes, Geoff,' Julia said dismissively, removing her coat. The cold air from the material drifted up into her nostrils with its captured smell of iced meadows. 'Delayed due to unfortunate, unavoidable circumstances.' She added, carrying the coat into the office. She didn't even glance at Carris, knowing Carris' explanation would come when Carris was ready.

'Besides, I think I'm allowed to be late once in a while. Wouldn't you agree, Carris?' Julia pushed into the office, which was no more than a cupboard. It was very tight in there, with only a sink, a toilet, numerous piles of books and an elephant's graveyard of curiously outmoded library publicity. Items that the Powers that Be in Bury St Edmunds had felt were a good idea at some point in time and then simply forgotten about. Suffice it to say, there was not even enough space for two people to pass each other. Julia was frequently forced into uncomfortable manoeuvres in order to keep her overly buxom frame from infringing on her young library assistant's personal space.

'Oh, yes,' Carris mumbled from the main library, 'occasional lateness due to unforeseen circumstances is certainly allowed.'

Julia clipped her coat onto the back of the office door. 'In fact,' she said as she lifted the kettle from the narrow bench beside the sink, swilling its contents, assessing its weight—yes, it would need filling. No surprise there. She flipped open the wide lid and held it under the faucet. 'I've only been late twice in my entire career of thirty years.' She glanced up to see that Carris had also entered the office, her thin, mouse-brown hair falling out of its clip. Her eyes all apologies.

'That's right,' Carris huffed breathlessly. 'Twice, today and...'

Carris wasn't old; she was in her mid-thirties, yet she had the demeanour of an octogenarian. Sometimes, it pained Julia to see someone go through life at quite the speed Carris did, throwing aside the years as if youth didn't matter.

'I'll get these,' Carris said, shuffling herself awkwardly to the far side of Julia. Their elbows and backs touched as they passed—inevitable in such a small space. They were used to it. Carris took the kettle, rested it once again on the shelf and flicked it on. All the while avoiding eye contact.

'It's no good, Carris,' Julia said gently, under her breath, so Geoff couldn't hear. 'You've got to be able to open up.'

Carris flustered. 'I know. I mean, I would, but I...' Awkwardly, she looked back out into the main library. 'The alarm.'

'You don't need to do the broom handle trick.' Julia said softly. 'Walk from the door to the back of the reception desk. There's enough time if you leave your bags outside.'

'Only just *enough time*,' Carris whispered, glancing down embarrassed at her hands, as if she had only taken delivery of them yesterday, and she truly had no idea what to do with her body.

'If the alarm goes off, it goes off,' Julia said pragmatically.

'Oh, Julia,' Carris sighed. 'I wish I had just one per cent of your confidence.'

Julia found herself disappointed Carris hadn't asked for more. Half of Julia's confidence would be a better start. If Carris were only after one per cent more volubility, there would be no hope for her. 'I won't be here forever, Carris.' Julia rested her hand gently on the younger woman's shoulder. 'I'll be retiring soon enough. A couple of years and you'll be on your own.'

'Oh,' Carris' face creased with worry. 'Don't Julia, let's not think of that now. It worries me. I just can't see that we've got long enough.'

It was, Julia knew, long enough. You could build a rocket and fly the thing to the moon and back in seven years, but that kind of mentality didn't apply to Carris, and Julia knew you always had to work with what you had. 'We probably need to practise again.' Julia smiled kindly. 'You'll be fine. Honestly.'

Julia's "honesty" seemed to reassure Carris. A small smile sparkled across her face. 'Tea?' she asked enthusiastically. Carris was always happy with a kettle.

'So, Julia.' Geoff's voice came from outside the office. 'You said you'd been late twice?'

Julia remonstrated herself mentally. She'd forgotten about Geoff—always a bad move. Every librarian knows you should never forget who's in your library. There was that awful case once over in Bromley; an old dear got stuck in the stacks for an entire Easter weekend. When they found her, she'd taken to eating the books. Although there were those who maintained she'd always had that unfortunate habit, and the escalation was simply to support an insurance claim.

'Late twice, exactly, Geoff. In thirty years,' Julia said as she re-entered the library. Sliding out the narrow desk drawer where she kept her name badge. 'Two occasions, and you were lucky enough to witness one. The first time, I had to deliver the Couldran baby.'

'Milly?' Geoff asked.

'That's the one. It was tricky, mind. I had no forceps, no medical training and no Wi-Fi signal. It was only fortunate that I knew Frank Millweed, who was living next door to the Couldran's before he built his bunker, had recently taken out a book *Surviving the Apocalypse in Uncertain Times*.'

'I would have thought an apocalypse has a degree of certainty to it?' Carris piped up from the office with unprecedented acuteness.

'Apparently not,' Julia called back. 'But the book did have a wonderful, illustrated section on delivering quadruped livestock. I felt confident that with a few allowances, I could re-work the practice to the application.'

Carris appeared at the doorway, a mug of piping hot tea in hand. 'You really are a wonder, Julia.'

Julia's heart softened. What Carris lacked on the adventure front could be overlooked in the face of her absolute and utter adulation. Being friendly with Carris was like having a very loyal dog that can talk, and seriously, as Julia headed towards sixty, she had to wonder—what more could a person want?

'Hmm,' Geoff said thoughtfully. 'Do you think there will be an apocalypse?'

'One day,' Julia said dismissively, going back to the front door so she could pick up the dropped books that everyone had stepped over.

'Only if there was...' Geoff nodded to himself zealously—a bad habit he had, as though he were continually chewing his words through and needed the physical exertion of numerous extra-large nods to masticate his vocabulary fully. 'If there was an apocalypse, I could sell the footage to LensStock.'

Julia sighed. She had no idea what or who LensStock was and, to be perfectly frank, no interest. She seemed to remember Geoff informing her that there were libraries which stocked film clips now. When he wasn't signing on, Geoff was an independent filmmaker. That was why he spent every hour of every day in the library—he had to research his ideas. This truly confounded Julia, since she couldn't imagine Geoff having any ideas, and if he did, those ideas were most likely bad and misconstrued. This was only borne out by Geoff's plan that, in the event of an apocalypse, he'd be able to sell the footage.

'I think you may be missing the point,' Julia said tactfully.

It was then that the door banged open, and the mystery as to why Julia was late that second time in her long career as library manager and why there had been a single police car at Hortishall Hall began to all fall into place because standing in the doorway with an aghast look on their face, mouth dropped open and trowel in hand, was Megan Keeble, head of The Allotment Allocation. From the look of absolute horror on Megan's face, something bad was clearly happening.

Geoff's eyes practically popped out of his head in excitement as he reached into his backpack and his trusty Panasonic GH4 mirror less camera—the one he'd picked up for a song from The British Heart Foundation's unwanted bin. 'The Apocalypse?' he asked, eager as anything.

For a moment, Megan Keeble was clearly knocked off guard. A beyond-puzzled look crossed her face. Then, she realised, of course, this was just Geoff, with his love of the cinematic medium and propensity for overly dramatic climaxes and conflict. In fact, suddenly, in the light of the apocalypse, this current news that Megan was about to deliver barely seemed important.

'Lord Hortishall...' Megan gasped, dropping the trowel from her fingers. 'He's dead.'

'Do you think they'll cut down the hedge now?' Mark Tanner wanted to know. It was understandable since he had a historical interest in the politics of leylandii.

The library had become very busy during the course of the morning. Julia had worked in the system long enough to know that it was always a sign of overcrowding when there were childless adults sitting on the beanbags. Not one person was checking out books. Even the Book Club, which met the first Monday of the month, showed no interest in discussing their current read. It was a shame because the novel had picked up all the awards - Pulitzers, Costas and Bookers. Since the Book Club followed a rigid trajectory, almost to the point of authoritarianism, if they didn't discuss it today, the prized novel would remain untouched on the shelf forever.

'The removal of the trees would depend on who wanted the hedge in the first place,' Clive Corpusty from The Ramblers Association, interjected sagely. 'If it was him or her.'

'Do we like her?' Ruth Silverling asked, crinkling the pretty nose on her pleasantly pudgy face. Ruth owned the dress shop in the village. As soon as the comment was out of Ruth's generously pink-painted lips, everyone couldn't help but wonder what insight Ruth had on Lady Hortishall. It must have been clear to all, even those oblivious to the continual fluctuations of a whimsical garment industry, that Ruth and Her Ladyship had very different approaches to fashion. Ruth favoured an overindulgence of material, giving an artistic, mysterious shape to the feminine form—an approach which delighted in the notion of being bigger and wider than the average women featured in the glossy magazines. In contrast, Lady Hortishall's clothing habits were a little more Chanel.

Before judgement could set its hungry teeth too far into the gathering, Julia thought it best to step in. 'I've always found Her Ladyship pleasant enough,' she stated cautiously. 'Although...' Julia could feel the baited air of anticipation fill the air. People loved an "although." But Julia, rising above the gossip, refused to satisfy. 'I was deeply fond of him.'

A wave of collective nods passed around the room, and the group relaxed under a tinge of relief as they upheld the pleasantries necessary in the wake of a death, despite the pressure.

'A lovely man,' Julia added.

Carris nodded eagerly. 'Julia here conversed with him several times. Isn't that right?'

Julia blushed as the congregation looked on appreciatively. Carris' statement was accurate, to a degree. Yes, Lord Hortishall and herself had spoken, but it wasn't exactly what Julia would have classed as *conversation*. Then again, sometimes, in a village such as this, conversation could be a difficult one to define.

It had been the Royal British Legion Fete on the first Sunday in June. The fete had always been held at Hortishall

Hall without fail, only once having been rained off. It was curious, really, because Julia could remember Lord Hortishall's exact words on every occasion they had met. The first time, he'd said, "Third door on the left," and on the second occasion, it was a little more. "Third door on the left, and mind the hot tap; these old houses have unpredictable plumbing." He'd said it all with that indulgent smile of his.

Julia had, in fact, never discovered, on any of her yearly jaunts, if there was a significant problem with the plumbing at the Hall since, in reality, the ladies' washroom had never been Julia's destination. No, Julia had other motivations each year at the fete. She had always known about the Hortishall library and its extensive collection of rare books —well, being a librarian, you tend to keep track of these things. It was the talk of many a library conference, and although never having been offered an official invitation, Julia did not take offence. It wasn't her style.

Instead, she took comfort in the will, always letting herself into the house while the fete was in full swing. The will was a true marvel. Not necessarily *will*, as in self-determination, although that did certainly come into it. Carris would never have dreamed of wandering around somebody else's property, but Julia found it perfectly plausible that a person might lose their way en route to the bathrooms. The Hall was, after all, a confusing labyrinth of rooms and corridors, and the Hortishalls were thankfully too classy, too proud, or too lazy to adopt the portable toilet conventions so popular with the big-house brigade. But the *will* which concerned Julia was of a different nature altogether. It was Lord Hortishall's Last Will and Testament, which Julia took enormous comfort in. Since in that will, Lord Hortishall stated that a quarter of all his books, rare antiquities and all, were bequeathed to the local library. She had this information, of course, in the strictest confidence. Librarians don't divulge secrets or sources. However, there is a lot of comfort to be drawn from knowledge. And in Julia's mind, nobody could dislike a man for an act of philanthropy on that measure, especially when that local library happens to be yours.

3

SPRING CLEAN

Staring nervously up at Julia, Carris pressed her ballerina-clad foot a little harder on the bottom rung of the ladder. 'Are you sure this is wise?' she asked, her vocal tone a note higher than normal. 'Shouldn't we wait till Geoff or somebody with a bit more counter-weight in their bottom half gets here?'

They had come in early on a Wednesday, the only day that the library had a half-day opening. The Wonderful Wednesday promotion had been rolling out for a few months now. The upper echelons of Library Management, sitting safe and sound behind their Monday to Friday desks, were rather partial to a new idea in order to shake things up. They'd circulated an announcement back in December. The main thrust was that Sunday would now pick up from where Wednesday would be left off. Sunday, so they said, was a great day to keep the doors open. Religious observances only took up an hour or so in the morning, leaving every other hour of the day available for reading. Therefore, a leisurely opening at 10:00 a.m. on the seventh day of the week was sure to make a difference to the much-coveted foot traffic targets—figures needed to impress the people with the purse strings.

Personally, Julia felt axing Sunday as a day of rest had socio-economic ramifications far beyond the swapping in and out of library titles. One casualty was poor Carris' love life. Everybody knew that Sunday was the go-to day for matters of the heart. Romantic love was not a necessity for Julia. Heading into her golden years, Julia was happy to confine that aspect of humanity to the romance shelves in the far corner of the library prefab. Besides, she would be retiring soon. Her Sundays were threatening to bounce back at her with the entire rest of the week, and as for religion? Julia partook spasmodically, more for the social side than from having any particular religious calling, and feeling that if there were a God, its omnipotence would be just as happy to have her cycling around the countryside, enjoying the workmanship, as sitting stiff and cold in one of the incense-smelling pews of the village church—St Mary Margaret of the Immaculate Conception. But Carris was still in her youth, and the regular sacrifice of a Sunday might well prove problematic. The poor woman barely had a chance to check her Tinder, let alone escape for a romantic trip to the beach or a rendezvous out of the county.

Unlike Julia, romance for Carris was a bit of a bit of a preoccupation. The small library had a more dynamic turnover of friends and lovers and rags to romance titles than any other library in the eastern region, and this was primarily down to Carris' unflinching efforts.

The only upside of Wonderful Wednesday was that it had been remarkably easy to grab Carris for a few extra hours on this fine February morning for a little re-organisation. Geoff and his additional weight were certainly not welcome. The man was a quagmire of unnecessary questions, none of them ever relating to the job in hand, and all having the unfavourable fallout of slowing down any kind of task that needed to be done. Besides, Julia might have been a big-boned woman, but she was well known for her balance—both in life and on a bicycle. Ladder climbing would not present a problem in the favourable conditions of a quiet library. It would be a good few hours until the door was pulled back and the Welcome sign set swinging above the steps.

Yet the slight vibrato Julia noted in Carris' voice indicated she was already worrying about the day ahead.

'Is it wise?' Julia repeated. 'Clearing a little space on the shelves? Absolutely. Carris, you just keep that foot pressed down firm.' She said as she slid a half-metre line of books directly from the shelf and into her wide, waiting arms. Her hands pressed the volumes together as though holding the ends of an accordion. Gracefully, she turned, attempting to pass the paperback volumes in one sweeping gesture down to the waiting Carris. Sadly, the manoeuvre did not go as intended. The neat line of books crumpled all too eagerly into the individual elements which they were, showering down like a plague of flapping frogs onto poor Carris' head.

'Oh, Julia.' Carris screamed, enveloped in a mist of pungent, sawmill damp and dust. 'Ew.'

Julia sighed, gazing down from her ladder at the book-battered Carris.

'Can't we just wait?' The young assistant's voice guttered into short bursts as she shook herself down. 'We don't even know how many books we're having to clear for.'

'A quarter,' Julia said, her voice a little short; they'd been through this before. 'One-quarter of the man's entire library.' She was secretly amazed, even with allowances for Carris being a little on the slow side, that she had to keep repeating the core facts—there weren't many. 'It's a big library, Carris. Bigger than ours.'

'Even if you included our office?' Carris asked with a genuine curiosity, which was marginally endearing.

'Our "office" is a bit of a misnomer, Carris. Surely, you've noticed it's nothing more than a pimped-up cupboard. Hortishall Hall, on the other hand, is an Elizabethan manor. Therefore, it has more room. You've only got to look at it from the outside to realise that everything behind those front doors is going to be way more bling and a lot less bottom-feeder barnacle.' She sighed. 'At a guess. I'd say the library at the Hall has a good 750 square feet more than we've got at our disposal.'

Carris looked confused. 'That's very precise.'

Julia shrugged. 'Well, give or take a foot or two.'

In fact, Julia knew there was no need to *give or take* even a large toe at the end of a size seven foot. She had measured the space one June at the annual Royal British Legion Fete. As the sound of Beatrice Bell's mechanical organ (always wheeled out for every occasion) chimed shrilly in the background, Julia had calmly placed her sensibly black Hush Puppy shoes, end to end in time with the high notes of the organ's canned trill—notes that had drifted across the verdantly stripped lawn of the manor and in through one of the (foolishly open) large leaded library windows.

'And another thing...' Julia stared up at the ceiling of the prefab-style book depositary—home to herself and Carris. 'Lord Hortishall's ceilings are a good deal higher than our own.'

When glancing down again, Julia realised she'd lost Carris, who was standing beneath the ladder looking more than puzzled.

'Higher ceilings,' Julia said, in order to get Carris up to speed with a push, 'means more books.'

'Oh!' Carris' face lit with all the excitement of a child given a puppy at Christmas, only to fall just as promptly. 'But what if Her Ladyship doesn't deliver?'

It was true; Julia hadn't expected a gap of some four months between the passing of Lord Hortishall and the arrival of the books. Wills get read pretty promptly after a body goes cold, and this will was absolutely crystal clear. When no books had been forthcoming, Julia, in her wisdom, had headed off to pay a visit to Reece Trumpington just as soon as a visit could be tactfully paid. Reece was Lord Hortishall's solicitor. He had an office above The Old Yarn—the village's only woollen shop. Julia knew where he lived, but a home visit didn't seem appropriate. In matters such as this, it was always a good idea to keep things business-minded. Reece had kindly got the document out of his safe. Julia had that way with people. Unusual, some might say, but she only had to ask, and people would normally be all too happy to do her bidding. She had a nice face, bonny, and although Julia was a person who might be prickly on occasions, she always cared. Fairness and caring were what Julia was all about. That was what people said when they spoke about Julia—because, let's face it, they did.

Reece, bless him, had gone through the whole two pages of the will with the curiously attentive library manager hanging off his every word, even though the tightly handwritten script was not always easy. Reece went through it line by line, exactly as he had done only weeks before with Her Ladyship. The writing, despite Lord Hortishall's slightly arrogant cursive, with its continental sevens, stunted s's, and carelessly uncrossed t's, was as clear as day: a quarter of all the books in his library would be on their way to Julia. Well, Julia, via the establishment of the village library.

'I don't think you realise quite how important this is,' Julia announced to Carris as she cautiously backed down the ladder. 'Those books are beauties, and we shall need to make space.'

Julia fondly remembered her multiple wanderings through the Hortishall collection. However, she wished she could remember these saunters without the uncalled-for addition of Beatrice's Organ, smashing its symbols and blowing its pipes. Sadly, the sound had ear-wormed itself into her memory, never to be washed out. Three years ago, Julia had invested in a pair of noise-cancelling headphones, the classical harmonies of Albinoni — her favourite composer, had accompanied her illicit wanderings. Fortunately, it was during the "Albi years" that she discovered her favourite treat. And this morning, standing back from the ladder into a sea of dropped books, in a fit of generosity and bonhomie (as well as niggled slightly by the apprehension that Carris seriously wasn't getting the point), Julia felt compelled to engage her young friend a little more on the subject of the Hortishall library and its wonders.

'You know, in that collection,' Julia said decisively, re-establishing herself soundly on the library floor. 'His Lordship had a first edition of a T. S. Eliot.'

'Oh,' Carris looked blank.

'*The Waste Land*.'

Carris glanced around nervously at the book chaos. 'Oh, Julia. Not to worry. We can get this cleared up in a tick.'

Sometimes, Julia despaired. 'No. It's a poem. *The Waste Land* by T. S. Eliot.'

Carris' eyes brightened in delight. 'Oh!'

'Exactly. The volume is an absolute beauty, Carris. It

even has a doodle of a butterfly on the inside of the front cover.'

'A butterfly.' Carris clasped her hands across her chest in genuine delight. She was a woman who liked to doodle herself, having taken life drawing classes for a few months in the village hall until she got tired of having to draw and re-draw the forever wrinkling lines of Mark Tanner—the naturist who had finally found a way to keep warm and get paid for his dearest pleasure.

'I know,' Julia said, a smile of remembrance at the first edition book spreading across her lips at the thought of the butterfly. 'I couldn't believe it when I saw it.' In truth, although she would not have described herself as a lepidopterist, Julia had returned every year to see that very butterfly etched in ink on the flyleaf. 'Personally, I wouldn't have had the great man down as a doodler. Eliot, I mean,' Julia said, just in case Carris had misunderstood and thought that it was Lord Hortishall who was *The Great Man* and perhaps had a penchant for library defacement. It was not uncommon for Carris to get the wrong end of the stick.

Carris nodded in agreement even though, most likely, she was not aware who Eliot actually was. Carris had been educated at the village school, and Julia knew allowances had to be made.

'But it all goes to show, Carris,' Julia said wisely, taking comfort in one of her favourite mantras: 'you never know the truth about people. They will always surprise you.'

'Oh, they do, they do,' the young library assistant echoed enthusiastically.

'Can you imagine,' Julia said, her eyes gazing off into the middle distance, 'if we had that very copy here in our library?'

'Oh, my goodness.' The younger woman's face broke into a wide bingo-smile. 'We'd even get the non-readers in.'

Surprisingly, Carris had hit the nail on the head. The non-readers were a constant cause of consternation for Julia. The bookworms were easily hooked. You barely had to feed them with new releases. They were forever happily mulling over back copies and imbibing the atmosphere. But this wasn't so for the non-readers, a group which had been steadily increasing since the proliferation of the time-waster handset culture took hold. It was the non-readers that were Julia's problem, and reaching them was a constant preoccupation. For Julia, it was certainly a case of individual salvation, but also something more—justifying the user targets held by the county. Without the counter situated above the library door, merrily clocking in each entrance and exit, targets could be innocently fudged, but since automation, things had changed. The pressure was well and truly on.

'You know I won't be here forever, Carris,' Julia said.

Carris glanced away awkwardly, avoiding eye contact.

'I shall retire, and you will need to take over. The library is important.'

Carris hooked her thin bottom lip under her teeth as she nodded.

'We have to make sure the service continues. If we don't hit our targets, the County Council will soon close us up. And there's a problem getting new readers since a village has a limited number of people.'

'Two thousand, three hundred and sixty-one.' Carris whispered softly. 'Sorry, sixty-three.' She corrected herself.

'Oh,' Julia said delightedly. 'Was it twins then?'

'No, there was one birth and one adoption.' She glowed. 'Busy week.' But her smile soon faded. 'Not that any of them will be reading anytime soon.'

Carris worked as the Parish Clerk on the first Thursday of each month. It had seemed a natural fit, being in charge of all the local records, what with also working at the library. Although it had cut down on time for a social life, Julia had half hoped romance might have bloomed with the young Parish Chair, Eddy Bright. A man aptly named, barely forty, single, financially stable, and tolerant—just about everything a woman like Carris could want. Sadly, so far, this was still not happening. The only plus side of Carris having taken the job appeared to be a statistical relish on the library assistant part, which, previously, Julia would not have thought cognitively possible. People will always surprise you.

'In order to survive,' Carris said slowly, unaware of Julia's brief reverie, 'we need the non-readers as well.'

'Exactly.' Julia smiled. 'But...' she stared up at the overly packed shelves and the overcrowded walls of the small, strip-lit, prefab library. 'We shall need to make room. The Eliot may be small, but re-housing a quarter of the Hortishall library, what with that additional square footage and the added increase in vertical shelving due to overly-generous Elizabethan headroom at the Hall is going to be an impossibility without a re-think.'

'You're right,' Carris said admiringly. 'This needs to be thought through.' She stared anxiously at the shelves ahead, suddenly realising the true implications of Lord Hortishall's will. 'And where will we even put the books that we take down?'

Julia hadn't really thought about this. Not in detail. 'We'll have to try and sell them off.'

'Increase library funds,' Carris said breathlessly, as though genuinely excited by the prospect. 'But they can't all stay in here. If the Hortishall books arrive tomorrow, what on earth will we do?'

Julia's forehead creased into furrows of thought. 'We'll have to store them somewhere. I could put them in my spare room until we work out a more permanent solution.'

'Great thinking,' Carris said, loading her arms with a line of books. 'I think it's best to do that now.'

'Wait.' Julia rested a hand on the young library assistant's elbow. 'There's too many to do them all at once. I won't be able to fit them all in my car.'

'Oh, Julia!' For some strange reason, Carris was suddenly looking over the moon. 'I can take them.' She squealed in genuine delight. 'I can take them all.'

'You'll never fit anything in your Midget.'

The small two-seater had been Carris' impulse buy of the previous year. An acquisition Julia had approved of. Only, like Julia's Smart Car, the Midget would not accommodate many books.

Bizarrely, Carris seemed undeterred. She was practically dancing around the library, turning in small, excited circles. 'I traded it in.'

This was news to Julia, and Julia didn't really like news creeping up on her in this way. It felt wrong. 'Traded in the Midget?' Despite its rather unbecoming banana-yellow paintwork, Julia had secretly rather envied Carris for her Midget.

'Exactly.' Carris squealed. 'Oh, Julia, I didn't know how to tell you, but I've most likely got room for all the books, every single one.' She glanced up at the packed walls as though drinking them eagerly in. 'I bought myself a campervan.'

'But you don't like camping.'

'I will if it's in a van.' Carris said, undeterred. 'It's a

wonderful thing—a Mazda Bongo. Barely bigger than a car and, Julia, don't you see...' Carris' wash-blue eyes glittered excitedly. 'This might be just the thing I need in order to kick start my love life. Nights away at the beach. The sound of the vast sea gently clawing at the shore's edge. He leans towards me and...'

'Enough.' Julia held one arm out towards her friend like a traffic warden.

'You get the picture,' Carris said excitedly.

Julia didn't actually want to *get the picture*. The thought was more than enough. Perhaps Carris had a point; a campervan was one step up from a beach hut and one step below a holiday cottage by the sea. Men love that kind of thing. However, this would most definitely knock Eddy Bright out of the running as a romantic interest. He might be single, financially stable, and tolerant, but he was also wide. There was no way he was fitting in Carris' Bongo.

'Well?' Carris was looking at Julia, all expectant.

'You didn't tell me,' Julia said.

Carris reached out, clasping Julia's hands between her own. 'I wanted it to be a surprise.'

Well, it certainly was that.

'We can even go away together. Lincolnshire's lovely.'

Julia couldn't see this happening on account of her having the same problem as Eddy.

'Besides,' Carris smiled up at her friend, 'I haven't got it yet. But I'm the highest bidder. I'm bound to win. The Midget's gone, so I'm on foot for the foreseeable, but the auction's only got two hours left to run. We could be moving books by tomorrow. Look...' Carris pulled her phone from her pocket, swiped it on and stared into the glow as if gazing into a crystal ball. 'Oh.' In an instant, every ounce of smile departed. 'Outbid,' she said, her voice curdling as she slumped awkwardly down on a pile of books. 'Oh Julia, I've been a fool.'

'No, Carris.' Julia reached out an arm, placing a hand gently on Carris' shoulder. Knowing that even if Carris had been a fool, confirming the fact would serve no purpose whatsoever.

'I thought I was bound to get the campervan, so I flogged the Midget in anticipation. Besides, I needed the money in order to go the full...Bongo.' Her voice narrowed into a squeak of despair.

Julia felt there was a word missing somewhere between Carris' "full" and the model of her car, but surprisingly, she got the picture.

'Now we'll never get the spare books over to your place.' And a large blue tear formed in the corner of Carris' pale blue eyes.

'Sorry,' a male voice interrupted—a voice suddenly embarrassed by the sight of tears. 'Oh, I'm so...so...sorry.' It was Des, the postman, standing awkwardly in the doorway with his ready apologies and his awkward frame.

He could be a good-looking man if only he remembered to stand straight. Only he never did. Julia had always thought that maybe it was the postbag dragging him down. It certainly wouldn't help.

'I...' Des stuttered, embarrassed. 'The door was...sorry.' He said sorry a lot, which made him very popular on a quiz night.

'Nonsense, Des.' Julia said. 'You're always welcome, although we're not quite open yet.'

Behind Julia, Carris sniffled, burying her face in the hastily administered leaves of a paperback.

'Is everything...sorry...is everything okay?' Des shuffled.

'Carris has had a bit of a shock.' Julia said sweetly,

handing Carris a tissue—Julia always kept one at the ready. Tissues were just part and parcel of a library manager's job.

'And I've let Julia down,' Carris sobbed.

A look of genuine concern flitted across Julia's face. 'No, Carris...' she said softly.

'I told her that she could borrow my Bongo, but it was never really mine.'

'Oh,' Des glanced awkwardly down at his feet. 'I've got a banjo if that's any good?'

This minor misapprehension only secured an opening of the floodgates on Carris' part, which in turn propped an avalanche of 'sorry' from Des.

Julia broke in quickly, her voice rising above the chaos. 'It's a van, Des. We needed a van.' Suddenly, it dawned on her like a shaft of God-given illuminated light showering down on something as important as a scattering of newly hewn commandments. 'A van,' Julia said, her voice level, '... and you're a postman, Des. So, correct me if I'm wrong, but you would have a van?'

4

NO-SHOW

It was late March before Julia concluded that decisive action was needed. They had endured over a month with the far wall of the library naked, staring down at them each and every day as if in judgment.

'Maybe we were too hasty,' Carris said, barely looking up from her morning's task of saving mutilated books. Her fingers deftly rebinding the chewed-up cover of a self-help paperback that advocated origami.

Julia's face creased into a frown. 'We had to do something. The library was already afflicted with a serious case of shelf congestion. We would undoubtedly have been compromised on the overtime front if the Hortishall collection had arrived all in one go.'

'Well, yes.' Carris paused for thought, drawing herself another line of Sellotape from the dispenser. There was certainly no chance of overcrowding now. The library felt decidedly bare.

'We could always bring *our* books back,' the younger woman offered brightly.

The hastily removed books were currently languishing

in Julia's spare room, safe and sound and away from the damp.

Julia sighed. If there was one thing she hated, it was doing something twice, whatever that thing might be. Going forward and going back had never been her style.

'Besides,' Carris exclaimed, an excited tone to her voice, 'now that I have the Bongo, transport's easy-peasy.'

Julia wished Carris would not revert to the "easy-peasy" adjective outside of the library's designated Toddler Time. Some years ago, Julia had foolishly employed a poet for the weekly Baby Singing Rhythm and Rhyme sessions. She had to reduce the sessions to every two weeks, when she'd noticed a dumbing down on Carris' adjective acquisition, coupled with an unfortunate inclination towards a tad too much alliteration. This was all bad, but when the onomatopoeia started to power in, Julia knew the poet had to go. The library might be a place of fun, but its principal remit should always be one of education and self-improvement.

However, on this particular morning, Julia chose to let Carris' "easy-peasy" slide in the light of the unabashed enthusiasm for life which had recently taken hold of the young library assistant. Carris had been overjoyed to win her bid on another Bongo—her fourth attempt. All in all, it had worked out well. Her eventual prize seemed preferable. This van was a real beauty: painted a tasteful metallic cream with tan piping in a rectangular strip on all doors. She had, however, ignored the subject of mileage. The mileage aspect had never made total sense to Carris, and now she seemed curiously reluctant to discuss the subject. But the vehicle's history was sound—one careful lady owner, much like Carris herself. The thing was immaculate inside and out, and this particular model even had a pop top, an addition

Carris was beside herself excited about. She'd popped it all over the village so the locals could take a look and marvel over the soothing, olive-green light which bathed the interior once the canvas was fully extended. Most of the men in the village seemed impressed that they were able to stand upright if positioned strategically beneath the highest point. Some didn't want to play ball on the measuring front, but many were fond of Carris and had, over the years, accrued enough library fines to their names, which Carris had habitually overlooked, and so they were happy enough to indulge.

'I don't think moving the books back is the answer,' Julia said, scrutinising the shelves.

'Then what, Julia?' Carris asked, giving a small flick of her startlingly thin, mouse-brown hair.

'The problem is the will. Lady Hortishall needs to be reminded.'

'Well,' Carris set her eyes back to her task—the refurbished books might well go some way to filling a hole in the recently vacated shelves, and the library doors would be opening soon enough. 'The will could easily have slipped Her Ladyship's mind. There's a lot to do when people die.' Carris said with unusual clarity. 'It came up at the council meeting just last week. They were wondering if it would be appropriate to hold the British Legion Fete at the Hall this year.'

'First Sunday in June?'

'Exactly. It's not so far away.'

'And the decision?' Julia was suddenly curious. In truth, she was having terrible pangs about the Eliot. It was no way certain that this particular volume would be dispatched from Hortishall Hall once the dispatching got itself underway. One last visit would have been a great relief, but Carris and the council were oblivious to Julia's feelings on this and countless other matters, and sadly, Julia couldn't work out an easy way to insist that the fete should go ahead without putting everyone's noses out of joint and their backs out of place.

'The Royal British Legion wrote to her.' Carris said, her mind still on Her Ladyship, rather than the Eliot or the promised books. 'The usual thing—expressing condolences, wishing her well, and saying that perhaps under the circumstances, they'd hold the fete elsewhere this year.'

There were three other big houses in the village—not as big as the Hall, but big enough for their owners to feel that they had a right to be hosting a fete of some description, and there simply weren't enough fetes, or enough reliable summer weather, to be shared around. No doubt someone would snap up the British Legion event, possibly even pay for the privilege. Julia had always felt that the actions of the wealthy were a mystery to everyone except themselves. In evidence, you only had to look at the jumpers they wore.

When she spoke again, Julia tried hard to keep the disappointment out of her voice. 'Very wise,' was all she could manage under the circumstance, regarding the proposed relocation of the fete.

'Eddy's idea.'

Julia noticed there was no frisson anymore when Carris mentioned Eddy's name, not one jolt of faultily wired electricity. As Julia had initially predicted, it must have been the Bongo that finished him off. The pop top would have served him adequately, but that extra weight he was carrying could have caused additional stress to the suspension. It was a shame, seeing as in all other aspects, Eddy would have been perfect. Julia took comfort in the fact that after one camping season, the

Bongo might well be back on the auction pages. Besides, she didn't want to dwell on Eddy or the campervan or Carris' love life and so returned her mind to the problem of the Hortishalls.

Surprisingly, considering her age, Julia had never had anyone die, or at least not anyone that she had needed to tidy up for afterwards. But, more than once, she had flicked through the volumes on bereavement in the Family Counselling and Self-Help sections of the library, and it was as plain as the pert but perfect nose on Julia's round ruddy face, that funeral admin did not end at the graveside. The council had acted tactfully in the aftermath of Lord Hortishall's expiration. However, Julia couldn't help thinking that her own situation was a tad different from that of the British Legion.

Her library was (in fact) part of the Hortishall bereavement mechanism—an integral aspect of the administration. Surely there should have been some communication by now? If it hadn't been for Reece's careless anecdotal introduction to his Lordship's will many Christmases ago, as they sat in the Dog and Duck after carols, munching on mince pies whilst Julia generously topped up Reece's sherry, and then Reece's kind illumination of the contents of the aforesaid will just over a month ago in his office over the Old Yarn, Julia would have been none the wiser as to the impending promise of an extra-large transit van full of valuable volumes.

'I think I'll head over to Reece's,' Julia said thoughtfully. 'Maybe get him to draft up a letter to Her Ladyship.'

'Give her a nudge?' Carris asked.

'Exactly,' Julia said, walking purposefully towards the office to retrieve her coat. 'He'll know the best course of action.'

'Well, I would think so.' Carris smiled brightly. 'If you can't find a book, find a person.'

This was a little saying that Julia and Carris passed backwards and forwards between themselves most days. It was surprisingly reassuring. It was reversible, too—if you can't find a person, find a book. However, in this particular case, only a person would do. Only a person could know the current state of play-up at the manor, and luckily, Reece was that exact person.

'And in the meantime,' Julia said, returning to the main body of the library, woollen hat and coat in hand. 'Perhaps we should...' Using her free arm, she cast a wide gesture around the room. 'Spread the books out a little.'

Carris stared up at the shelves. 'Spread?'

'Yes, Carris. I think many of our shelves are too overbooked. In fact, when I look at them now, the spines are so tightly packed, my brain can barely process all the titles.'

'Oh, I know,' Carris replied eagerly, a woman whose brain was well known to be a little slower with any kind of processing. 'It makes me feel giddy sometimes.'

The thought of a giddy Carris was not an image Julia welcomed, and she knew instantly that action was called for. 'Then, since we currently find that we have the shelf room, perhaps it's best to disperse the entire library within the available space. We need a paradigm shift here.' This was a term Julia had picked up from her annual training sessions at the Library Management Centre, where they'd often insisted that the library service was no longer just a place for books. With the advent of technology, a paradigm shift had occurred in the need for borrowing and the role of the book provider. Julia kept quiet on the matter, but didn't agree. She liked books and felt the principle of borrowing had been going on since the hunter-gatherer times, so she saw no need for a change now. However, Julia also liked the term paradigm shift. It felt big and dynamic, and therefore she had relished the opportunity to put it into action in her own sweet way.

'Rather than empty shelves, Carris, and not enough books, we must think of our literature as being perfectly placed. Like a Picasso, which needs a little space in order for people to appreciate it fully.' She glanced around, taking the library in—one wall of empty shelves and three walls bulging like racks of beer barrels threatening to explode. 'So, we just redistribute what we have.' She nodded, satisfied. 'A conscious decision.'

'Oh, I do like that, Julia,' Carris said brightly, a look of excited awe giving her cheeks a small pink flush before the flush clouded with practicalities beyond Carris' paygrade. 'And if the books don't arrive?'

Julia shrugged, slipping her arms into her coat. 'We rethink. We action another kind of sea change.' She'd learnt that one on the course as well. It was proving to be that kind of morning. For years, you used nothing that the library service had taught you, and then all at once, everything fell into place. 'But for now,' Julia said, pulling her hat down over her greying curls. 'Let's just work with what we have.'

This last nugget of wisdom was something head office had never advocated to Julia - or any of the many other district librarians - as a course of action. Not once had it been whispered in any course or shouted out in Helvetica font via the library's internal mail system, and yet this was the one phrase by which Julia lived her life.

Initially, Reece had been reluctant to send a letter to Her Ladyship. He felt the personal touch, in situations such as these, was better. So Reece proposed he talk to her and mention the promise of the books. Julia knew for a fact that Reece was up at the Hall most days. She saw his peacock-blue Lexus parked outside the manor as she rode her bike past the gates each day. Yet, months passed, and Julia found herself frustrated by the lack of action. She began to get the sneaking suspicion that, left to Reece, the matter of the books would never be broached. However, she could see that there was a predicament here. You didn't need a law degree to know that the first rule of being a solicitor was no blabbing. Undoubtedly, Julia knew there would be a fancier and more legal term for it, but blabbing would be what they meant, and Reece had blabbed on two occasions. He alerted Julia to the contents of the will and then showed her the thing in his office. It appeared that Reece was no longer in a blabbing mood.

There was a possibility that this could all end badly. She had prompted Reece to remind Her Ladyship too many times and had noticed recently that the solicitor's library books were going overdue. She got the distinct impression that she was being avoided. People often had to pick sides in life, and Reece was only human (despite the rumours which had been quashed when he attempted to take liable action). Julia was all too aware that a bottle of sherry and a mince pie were not the same as regular wages. Regular wages can topple any ethical considerations that might have seemed prominent after a glass of fortified wine in the comfort of the Dog and Duck, with the flakes of the Women's Institute mince pies still hot on one's lips.

If Julia approached Her Ladyship about the books, there was a strong chance Reece would be out on his ear, struck off, and discredited. Her Ladyship would want to know how Julia had heard about the will.

Julia had always felt that being the manager of a small community library came with a certain responsibility. You didn't necessarily have to like all your fellow men/women/non-binary neighbours, but you did have a duty of care. Julia knew she couldn't dunk poor Reece in the hot water. She would have to find another way of confronting Her Ladyship without dragging in the solicitor.

~

'Wouldn't you rather have a card?' Carris said, gazing down at Julia, who was sitting neatly at her desk, pen in hand. A sheet of freshly bought paper was laid out in front of her. 'There are some lovely ones of the carousel.'

Julia had never approved of the decision to sell items through the library. Pens, notebooks and book bags she could understand. These had a literary and research connection fitting for a library, but greetings cards had always seemed a step too far.

'I think cards are a little contrived,' Julia said, wishing Carris would get on with a task which didn't involve standing quite so close to the desk.

'Contrived?' Carris' features dropped. Her face paled. She looked quite horrified.

'Yes, Carris, *contrived*,' Julia said, suppressing a yawn. She had been up all night worrying about the best way to approach this situation, and the last thing she needed now was a philosophical discussion on the nature of stationery. However, looking up and seeing Carris' blank features, she realised the conversation was necessary. 'A card,' she said, releasing her pen, letting it roll across the desk a little. 'Is already doing half the work—it's saying sorry, or thank you, or offering condolences.'

'And that's a problem, why?' Carris said, one recently tattooed eyebrow rising in an arch like a seagull.

'The card is saying whatever it happens to be saying on behalf of the greeting card industry. Therefore, it is not genuine.'

'Oh.' Carris' forehead creased into a series of waxy lines as perfectly parallel as a stave on a sheet of music. 'I sent out a get-well to Milly Winterbottom just the other day. She's had a terrible time with her lachanophobia.'

Now it was Julia's turn to look curious.

'Fear of vegetables,' Carris said helpfully.

Julia's lips quivered in a wry smile. 'Milly is eight, Carris. Having a fear of vegetables is just called fussy eating. No need to invoke classical civilisation to justify it.' She sighed wearily as she reached under the desk for one of her go-to favourite manuals—titles she always kept close at hand. Book staples, as every day as paracetamol would be to a pharmacist, most of humanity's ailments and quests boiled down to a few similar themes.

'This would be much more appropriate than a card with a lot of well-wishes.' She handed Carris the book she always prescribed in such instances: *Veggie Ventures* by Clementine Cooke—the veg whisperer. 'There's a truly innovative idea in there for what to do with a glut of aubergines,' Julia said flatly.

Carris took the book, placing it next to the Millionaire Romance she'd already bagged from the Quick Pick carousel. 'Thank you, Julia. I'm not completely sure what I'd do without you. I'll make sure she gets it.'

Having dismissed the distraction of greeting cards, Julia returned her focus back to Lady Hortishall's letter.

'So,' Carris said. 'Wasn't that just the biggest stroke of luck?'

Julia halted once again, raising her pen from the paper. 'Luck?'

Carris grabbed herself an armful of books from the book drop and proceeded to place them back on the shelves. 'That Lord Hortishall told you about his will.'

Julia glanced awkwardly down at the still blank page. 'Yes,' she said, keeping her voice level.

'I mean, if you hadn't been told, we would have never known.'

'Exactly,' Julia said, still not raising her eyes.

'And Lady Hortishall having so much on, she could have easily forgotten.'

'Quite so.' Julia had an uncomfortable feeling that her eye might begin to twitch. Suddenly, she was feeling very hot under her navy angora sweater and wishing she had worn something lighter.

'Yes,' Carris continued. 'Very lucky. When did he mention it to you? At the fete?' Carris asked, curious.

Julia knew she had to turn this around and take possession of it. She needed to put one of those Sea Changes in place that she admired so much. 'Carris,' Julia gave her young library assistant a firm, controlled look. 'Where else could I have talked to Lord Hortishall?'

Carris smiled, slipping Dostoyevsky's *Crime and Punishment* neatly back into the Classic Fiction section under D. 'Oh Julia, you do make me laugh.' She said with a trill. 'I don't think the man ever came out of the Hall. Thank goodness for the British Legion Fete, eh?'

Thank goodness, indeed. Thanks to the fete, Julia had managed to avoid telling an out-and-out direct lie. This was a relief since another of Julia's favourite mantras, one she lived her life by and encouraged in others, was that nobody liked a liar.

'Do you think it should be signed yours truly, with sympathy or sincerely?' Carris asked as Julia's pen glided over the writing paper.

'The ending's not important,' Julia said, signing off with her name, title, and the library's contact details. She made sure these details could be easily read but stopped short of including a stamped addressed envelope, although she was tempted. 'It's just a reminder.' Julia said, taking the letter and folding it neatly in half before slipping it into its tasteful sky-blue envelope—blue, so it could not be overlooked amongst all the other plain white missives—blue, so that Lady Hortishall would be aware that this was important and personal—blue so that Her Ladyship would know that the sender was serious. The promise of the books would not be forgotten.

5

THE REPLY

To Whom It May Concern—that was how the letter was addressed.

It was a hastily scrawled dash of ink sitting beneath the Hortishall Hall crest—two eagles. Were they kissing or fighting? The attitude of the eagles was unclear and possibly beside the point. What was evident was the stark contrast between the embossed ironed-in-place crest, sitting proud as a line of brail upon the thick white wove of Her Ladyship's personal stationery, and the careless penmanship on Lady Hortishall's reply. Penmanship, it must be remembered, was acquired courtesy of rigorous processing through some of the fanciest public schools on the planet.

'Oh,' Carris winced from the opposite side of the mug-ringed table, leaning forward a little to get a closer look at the blue spider-mess tangle of words.

It was Wednesday morning, and instead of heading straight to the library, Julia and Carris had pencilled in a detour via Sal's Snippy Biscuit—the coffee shop on the green. Sal was the new owner occupant, and everyone in the village liked to support one of their own. Knowing all too well that in a rural community, if a new business attempts to take its first fledgling breath, it needs all hands at the cradle —a case of use it or lose it. Carris and Julia had even devised a rotation schedule. They made a point of dropping in just about everywhere they were needed at a pre-planned date each month.

Cautiously, Carris traced her index finger over the handful of words on the letter in front of her. 'I get your point, Julia. It is a little abrupt.' She conceded. 'But maybe Her Ladyship didn't catch your name?'

Julia knew this could not be the case. She had been very careful to write her details clearly. Besides, Lady Hortishall's reply had arrived in response to Julia's fifth, plainly written dispatch. It was now May. Lord Hortishall had been under the ground, cooling off, for a good seven months. Yet still, not one single volume of His Lordship's vast catalogue had managed to flaunt its covers past the swinging library welcome sign and through the doors of the village library.

'Well,' Carris pushed back on her chair with a small sigh. 'Her Ladyship does say here that she will get the books over to us.'

This, in truth, was the sole content of the letter. This, and the "To Whom It May Concern." Julia couldn't help but feel that the people of the village deserved more and that the lack of bonhomie suggested a veiled snub.

Sensing tension, Carris rubbed the back of her neck awkwardly, pulling subconsciously at strands of baby hair, which appeared to spend every waking hour plotting an escape mission from her scrunchy. 'Maybe we should have offered to pick the books up?' She said nervously.

'I did.' Julia replied, stirring her mochaccino way more than was necessary, disrupting the artisan "S" for Sal, which had been artfully engraved in the foam, before trying, unsuccessfully, to reconstruct it.

'Oh, Julia.' Carris pulled her bamboo straw out of her handbag and slipped it into her large matcha espresso.

Despite herself, Julia felt an involuntary eye roll kicking into action. 'You don't need the straw, Carris. Sal's taken over. The beans are safe.'

For anyone not residing in the village over the past two years, this statement may have seemed cryptic. It was worthy of something one might send off to Baker Street in the hope of a quick decoding. Yet, for the locals, it would have made perfect sense. Sal had recently taken over the small coffee shop on the green from Ben Wiseman, a crook if ever there was one. After only six months of Benjamin serving his beans, the locals became a little disconcerted that their teeth were becoming stained. Stains were the sort of thing that nobody wanted to mention. Keen for a quick, discreet, whiten and polish, those who could afford the price ticket started taking their diminishing smiles to the Hygienist in the neighbouring village—Olivia Dentlow.

It was a good two months before Gwyn Thomas, a retired schoolteacher living with her six cats in one of the Tide cottages on the green, began to suspect that all was not well with Benjamin's Morning-Special blend. A keen Christie fan, Gwyn had read every single book the infamous crime writer had ever written and saw herself as a bit of a sleuth. Some said Gwyn was obsessed. Others claimed she could put most people to sleep in under half an hour when engaged on her subject of choice. Whatever the case, Gwyn's aptitude for understanding the criminal mind was a marvel. She was always highly sought after for quiz nights down at the Dog and Duck, especially after they introduced their True Crime line of questioning.

Possibly, this mild celebrity status had gone to Gwyn's head. But when her habitually bright ivories started growing three shades dimmer, Gwyn engaged valiantly in the mystery. Deduction was needed. Gwyn quizzed herself, just as Miss Marple herself might have interrogated a witness. Was there anything different about her routine? She quickly narrowed it down to the coffee shop. It was then that she started to notice the clues—pride of place on Ben Wiseman's noticeboard was a flyer for the Dentlow Dental Practice in the next village. Once she was on the right track, the trail seemed clear—why would a coffee house be offering referrals for dental treatments directly underneath listings for bean blends? Even more suspicious, there was a 20% discount when you used the code Lovely Dentist Woman, and as Gwyn announced one quiz night after a glass too many sherries, Lovely Dentist Woman was practically an anagram of Olivia Dentlow and Benjamin Wiseman. She used 13 letters from Olivia Dentlow and 15 from Benjamin Wiseman, but John McTavish, who emceed the quiz nights, brought Gwyn up on her deduction. The anagram was baggy. Lovely Dentist Woman only had 18 letters. Ben and Olivia had 28. But by this time, nobody cared. It was obvious to all that—Wiseman's beans were causing the yellowing smiles of the locals, and attractive young Olivia Dentlow was in cahoots.

Many of the villagers were keen to take a class action against the dastardly duo. According to PC Gary Mumblings, this particular scam even had a name—the Coffee and Chompers Con. It was happening every day up and down the country. Dental colleges were warning their students to be on the lookout for coffee shop owners offering get-rich schemes and free lattes. Julia did wonder if PC Mumblings was exaggerating slightly, feeling that he often used the deep, dark blue cut of his uniform to give his thoughts a legitimacy that they perhaps did not deserve.

Luckily, the item had been included on the Parish Council Agenda, and local solicitor Reece Trumpington was called in to speak. He advised the gathered community that on no account should they consider taking legal action against the Smile Robbers, as the couple had been dubbed locally. The matter was dropped. Only weeks after the Parish Council meeting in which Reece had urged restraint, Benjamin sold the coffee shop to Sal for a song.

Julia could have clarified the Benjamin/Olivia situation if asked. She had noticed via the inter-library loan system that Wiseman had been borrowing exactly the same books as Olivia. It was a mixed bag, but they were reading the same things. He'd borrow *A Room with A View* for one week and two weeks later, the book would be pulled out by young Olivia. This had been going on for years. It didn't take a degree in library management to know that people who read together "play" together. Yet Julia kept her own counsel. The librarian's code was one of non-disclosure.

'Let's be pragmatic here.' Carris said, bringing Julia back to the coffee shop with a bump. 'Her Ladyship says she'll get the books to us, and she will. Apart from being offended that she didn't know your name, Julia, I can't see what you're worried about.' The younger woman smiled benignly. 'There's nothing to worry about. Let's face it, your name is legend.'

Julia tried hard to stop herself from blushing, but she found the reassurance curiously touching. It was good to be known and liked. Did Lady Hortishall really matter? It wasn't as if the two women were ever going to be friends. Lady Hortishall was partial to biographies of the aristocracy. The only genre Julia had never touched since Julia had noticed that the aristocracy tended to have a high opinion of themselves—an opinion that their ghostwriters were seldom able to control. Therefore, the two women would have nothing to converse about.

'Everyone loves you.' Carris said gently. Mistaking Julia's silence for hurt. 'I have no idea what I'd do without you and the library, Julia, guiding me forward in my life.'

Julia had no idea either. Carris was well known for her poor direction, and this was another source of worry. They'd fixed the Bongo, making sure to purchase the best sat nav known to man. But there was no sat nav for life. Someday, Carris was going to have to stand on her own two feet.

'Most likely, Lord Hortishall never mentioned you were close.' Carris said, pursing her lips and blowing down her bamboo straw before taking a sip of her hot coffee.

'Not so much *close*,' Julia cleared her throat awkwardly. 'But we had spoken.' She was always unwilling to own a lie; an omission was far more favourable.

'Exactly.' Carris raised both arms in a wide, dismissive shrug. 'And perhaps Her Ladyship was jealous. It doesn't take much.'

Julia felt it would probably take a lot more than "Third door on the left" and "Mind the hot tap; these old houses have unpredictable plumbing." But then again, you never can tell with people.

'Besides,' Carris said lightly, reaching across the table and taking Julia's hand into her own. 'Receiving the Hortishall books is a real coup for the library, and it's all down to you.'

For once, Carris was right; if it hadn't been for Julia being hot off the mark, there was no doubt Her Ladyship would have forgotten the books. Now, at least, the promise would be fulfilled. Julia had it in writing. Scrappy writing, but writing it was. So why did Julia feel an overwhelming sense of doom? She glanced out of the windows onto the green, its far edges trailing away onto the common and into the hills. May was always her favourite time of year. Out of all the seasons, it was the one which held all the promise. One could never be bored with May. The hedgerows were bursting. The horse chestnuts swayed their triangular towers of white flowers, lining the edge of the road as though decorated soldiers on parade. All was at peace.

Across the way, Julia could see Pierre, in his chef's whites, standing on the doorstep of his restaurant, chatting with Megan Keeble. Megan's quirky Citroën van, which looked as if it had been made of a strip of corrugated iron, was parked at a jaunty angle on the curb. With its doors unlocked, Julia could see contents of crate upon crate of organic veg spilling out onto the pavement. The produce was so fresh it looked as though it had been freshly polished that very morning.

Glancing in the other direction, Julia could see Ruth Silverling intent on her task of dressing the window of her clothes shop. She fixed a floaty botanical print to a plus-size mannequin with genuine joy, which seemed childlike and curiously touching.

Then there was the Harmony Hut. It was just a village hall—nothing fancy, and another prefab. Although, it was older than the library, and it had more intricate detailing and a sloped brown roof that had the look of strips of plasticine. Painted green gables adorned the door, and the entire building stood on a foot or two of bright red-brick plinth.. It housed the Parish Council once a month. There was weekly yoga and fortnightly mother and baby, but every Wednesday evening, the hall would host the choir. Its sound filtered across the green of an evening, adding to the feeling of peace and tranquillity that the village enjoyed. As Julia watched, Clive Corpusty, the caretaker, ambled over, keys in hand, to check all was well at the hall. He checked that there were towels in the bathroom, bleach down the toilets and enough paper on the holders to service around twenty-five people of mixed and indiscriminate genders. People in the village cared.

Julia had never thought she'd stay as long as she had, but the community had welcomed her in and taken her to its heart. Then why, oh why, in such a perfect setting, with her bike parked up outside, blatantly unlocked, and the sun shining and the community going about its work. Why, with the promise of the books she so wanted, written on paper as thick as Moses' tablets themselves, why did she feel so unsettled? She would take delivery of the books, sell the ones not needed and put the money into the library funds. This would help keep the system afloat. After all was shelved and banked, she'd start getting ready for the handover. She wasn't entirely sure Carris was up to being library manager, but there was no one else Julia would rather see do it.

Besides, she raised her mochaccino to her lips and took a long hard sip, careful to avoid attracting herself a moustache; the fete would soon be happening—the first Sunday in June. Perhaps this would be the watershed when Her Ladyship got her books in order. Perhaps Lady Hortishall would invite Julia into the library, and they could discuss requirements. Maybe Julia would get to see the Eliot one last time.

'Of course,' Carris said sadly, taking her straw from her coffee and licking its foamed end with relish. 'It is a shame about the Royal British Legion.'

Julia felt a lump in her stomach, like cold porridge after

a night on the town. For a moment, her words seemed to fail her. Luckily, Carris didn't notice.

'The council wrote to Her Ladyship saying they'd love to hold it there this year.' Carris tutted, raising her eyes heavenward in resigned dismay. 'It was a total disaster last year.'

The Old Vicarage had taken the fete over. Although, it was a home now—not a vicarage at all. However, the Old Vicarage assumed control of the fete and were given permission to retain the name under the condition that no witchcraft would be practiced in the house or the gardens. This had been written into the deeds so there could be no confusion. Luckily, the owner had no interest in the occult. It had been bought from the church back in the eighties by Beatrice Bell—the lady with the mechanical music makers. The organ wasn't Beatrice's only large-scale automated device. Beatrice and her husband Salvatori collected large junk just as greedily as some collect stamps. They also had a phone box growing out of the garden and had planted a red double-decker bus. The council had spent many years trying to get it removed, to no avail. Salvatori was an opera singer, and when Beatrice's machines weren't clanking out tunes, Salvatori was singing *O Mio Babbino Caro* in everybody's ears. That had been the problem with the fete. Billy Bryce, always a bit of a wide boy even though he was now in his forties, claimed he'd had a ringing in his ears ever since, and not in a good way. Luckily, Reece, the local solicitor, was on hand again, and always pragmatic and quick to act. Reece had squashed an insurance claim for tinnitus. Telling Billy and anyone else who thought this might be a good line of income that it was almost impossible to prove where a person would pick something like tinnitus up. The upshot had been favourable, on some fronts at least. It had been noticed that Beatrice's pipes seemed to get a bit quieter. But life was like a seesaw, where there was an up, there was a down, and on the downside, in the face of litigation, the Royal British Legion Fete had become a bit of a hot potato. So the council had been counting on Her Ladyship to step up to the plate once more.

'And?' Julia asked, barely able to suppress her excitement. 'What about the summer fete?'

'Well,' Carris sighed languidly, twiddling once again with those baby hairs at the nape of her neck. 'Her Ladyship's reply...' She paused awkwardly.

'Yes?' Julia sat forward in her seat.

'It was a little wordier than your...' she glanced down at the letter on the table, "To Whom It May Concern."'

'But, Carris what, what did the letter say?'

'Exactly?' Carris shivered, like a rabbit in the headlights, uncomfortable under pressure.

Julia waved her arms dismissively. 'The general gist.'

'Well,' Carris' eyes narrowed as though conjuring up the epistle to her brain. 'It said that Her Ladyship felt the village had received more than enough support from the Hall over the years and that, due to the circumstances, it would be best to find alternative avenues.'

6

THE FETE

It was the first time the Royal British Legion Fete had been held on the green since the war. 1945 had witnessed a brief twelve-month stint in which the Hall had been used as a convalescent home for the wealthy but wounded. There were rumours that Lord Hortishall's grandfather, Roland, whose idea it was to use the Hall in this way, had been keen to marry off, what he described as his "unfortunately, bookish daughter," Elois. Hoping to introduce the retiringly shy lass to someone of substance between the bedpans. Armed with a large red cross on a white apron, Eloise had briefly taken her focus away from the library and Renaissance poetry that she loved briefly enough to fall for a young man with a stiff gait and heavy lisp. Her father's plan had worked, and as luck would have it, the young man with the slithering consonants and knobbly knees returned Eloise's affections—no one can resist a ministering angle. Eloise's father gleefully packaged his daughter up in a white dress, stuck the family tiara on her head, and married her to this minor member of the aristocracy with a speed which was startling. It was from Eloise's union that, in the 1950s, the recently deceased Lord Hortishall had been born—born, already worrying about the inherited plumbing of such a major manor, along with the mindboggling logistics of repairing halls and corridors that no one used anymore, on a household budget that had been halved, quartered and finally left in a state that no longer had a commonly recognised fraction.

It should be noted that the green was not an ideal place for a fete. Despite its idyllic roadside boundaries of horse chestnuts and the small but perfectly formed pond, stippled with yellow flag iris' and frequented by dragonflies, the problem with the green was that its southernmost corner tapered seamlessly into the common—a wide body of rural land. It was bucolic and truly enchanting. Therefore, people tended to amble off with their candy floss, ice creams and clotted cream fudge, tempted by the common's wide vistas, rare bee orchids and the gracefully beckoning arms of Queen Anne's lace. In short, despite being at the very centre of the village, the green itself had no way of fixing people in place, and a fete was the kind of event that needs to keep people fixed.

In their wisdom, the Parish Council marked off the meeting of the green and the common with a low wall of hay bales. These would serve as a natural barrier as well as additional informal seating. This was the kind of rustic improvisation an event like this excels in. It looked as though, despite all, the day would be a success.

In a similar pragmatic approach, Julia put aside her disappointment that this year she would be unable to visit the Hall for a surreptitious gander at the Eliot. Circumstances were beyond her control, and if the fete had to be moved, Julia knew she must also simply make the best of it. Besides, the location shift was not Julia's prime concern. It was now June, the first Sunday of the month, and the promised books from the Hortishall collection were still MIA. Missing in *apathy*, Julia felt, rather than in *action*, although the result appeared to be the same. This, too, appeared to be beyond her control. There was simply no way the library manager could compose another letter to Lady Hortishall. Five letters constituted stalking. Julia had managed to glean this useful nugget of information from PC Mumblings without having to tell him the specifics of the case or admit to the fact that she happened to be cycling past Hortishall Hall most weekdays and even occasionally at the weekend. Although this journey was made in total innocence, even Julia felt that it could be construed as odd behaviour since it was not the quickest route from her own door to her place of work.

Julia's only hope for communication, she reasoned, was that perhaps Her Ladyship would grace the fete with a visit. The Hortishalls had only ever missed one British Legion Fete since they'd been joined in wedded bliss way back in the seventies. In fairness to Lord Hortishall, he had missed that one occasion on account of him being unavoidably dead, and in fairness to Her Ladyship, it was widely supposed that she was grieving. She wept poetically into her monogrammed handkerchief as Beatrice Bell's organ was controversially shattering the peace of the village along with a fair few eardrums.

This year, surely she would appear. The council had even asked Lady Hortishall to cut the ribbon of the maypole at the opening ceremony. She'd replied on her embossed, heavy stationery that this would not be possible. No reasons were given, but the council's offer had been declined. Yet still, Julia did not lose hope of a serendipitous conversation with Her Ladyship at the event. Reasoning, there was a difference between a formal engagement of ribbon cutting and a pleasant wander upon the green to purchase a little local produce. Everything one wanted could be found at the annual fete, from cakes that make your mouth water to cutters shared freely from everyone's gardens. It was, in fact, a well-known fact that Her Ladyship was rather partial to Blythe Nithercote's lavender honey. Blythe only ever sold her lavender collection at the fete. Therefore, it might be readily deduced that if the weather was fine and honey stocks at the Hall were low, Lady Hortishall would be coming for a wander.

Besides, a replacement had been found for the opening ceremony. The Parish Council had asked Julia if she would do the honours that year of cutting the ribbon and saying a few words. Julia was known for her ability to hold an audience and often found herself wheeled out in order to deliver a line or two when a celebratory or dignitary discovered themselves out of sorts. Julia herself was delighted with this arrangement, as it meant she wouldn't have to tie herself into running one of the stalls. If tied to a table, on spotting Lady Hortishall, Julia would have had to keep her eye on the punters and her hands on the float. If free to breeze from stall to stall, Julia might easily wander up to Her Ladyship for a quick stroll and a chat. Mentioning the books would not be stalking, simply conversation on a pleasant summer's day. Nothing could be simpler. The only thing that could put a spanner in the works would be if the weather was poor. If the heavens opened, the fete would be a sad affair of soggy cakes, wet hair and everyone smelling more like old dogs than the more preferable country garden. However, this particular first Sunday in June opened like a gift over the common. There was a perfect blue sky, with not a cloud in sight, a chorus of bird song, and the sound of happy villagers setting up their trestle tables as they argued good-naturedly over having the best spot.

The band started promptly at 11:00 a.m. They'd been practising all year, which was always a surprise, but despite the missing notes and flat flatulates of the tuba, everyone smiled and sang along if they recognised a word or a phrase that they could sink their teeth into. After the ribbon cutting, Julia made a trawl of the stalls. Her Ladyship hadn't arrived, but then midday on a Sunday was still early. The day was young. The last trestle tables wouldn't be taken down until 4:00 p.m. when the hog roast would be wheeled out, and somebody buoyed up by bonhomie would be sure to sponsor a keg of cider from the Dog and Duck. There was more than enough time for Her Ladyship to arrive.

The green had been newly mowed for the occasion, and the smell of cut grass filtered through the air. Julia wandered past the tea tent; its white marque was adored with triangles of bright bunting, fresh from the needles of the WI.

'Julia.' A woman called and waved as she walked past. 'Can we tempt you?' Marta Harris called coquettishly, angling a display stand of cut sandwiches in Julia's direction.

'I'll be back.' Julia said. A promise she did not intend to keep. If she sat for one moment inside that tent with its gently billowing white canvas and diffused summer light, she knew she would be lulled just as surely as a lotus eater. She'd have pot after pot of English Breakfast tea to wash down the sandwiches, iced cakes, and strawberries and cream. She'd sit there, letting the chatter of the crowd, the laughter and the clinking of the cups wash over her. From far away, she would hear the muted loudspeaker announcing the shows of the day, ticking off the events as they fell: the dog show, the fancy dress, the wellington boot throwing and the carrying of the spouse. It would all wash over her, and she would forget that this might be her last opportunity to remind Her Ladyship of the missing books. All would be lost inside the billowing flaps of the tent. She needed to keep her wits about her.

She passed a small cluster of owners and dogs, preening themselves, adjusting collars and coats before the show began, and the dogs would need to be looked too. After pocketing herself a couple of jars of lavender honey, Julia stopped briefly by Carris' table. Carris was running the Hit the Rat stall. It was a tried and tested favourite. It involved a length of drainpipe, a toy rat, and a large, intimidating baton. Standing on a chair, Carris had to drop the toy rat down the pipe. Then, someone at the end, someone who had paid fifty pence for the privilege, would attempt to hit the rat with the stick as it shot from the drainpipe at speed. Since Carris had forgotten to go to cash-and-carry, she'd been forced to improvise with the rules a little. Normally, a hit of the rat would be awarded with a lollipop. Today, the lollipop wasn't happening. Today, a direct hit would secure the lucky punter with another go. In fact, they would get another go until their arms ached and they gave up. Not one parent had complained that this was a bad idea. In fact, quite the reverse. As young Luke Thomas fell to the floor on his twenty-fifth attempt, his parents looked delighted. Luke was a boy known for his boundless energy. One lollipop and the lad would have been fizzing into the following week.

Julia had always thought that life was odd like that. Mistakes could often turn out to be triumphs. Perhaps Carris would get allocated the stall again next year as well. Truth be told, there was always something a little juvenile about the stalls which Carris was called upon to run. Despite living in a village, rather surprisingly, Carris could do nothing on the artisan front—no baking, needlework or painting. She couldn't decorate shells, turn wood, make rugs out of rags or cobble together necklaces using nothing more than bottle tops and a pair of intricately small pliers, as so many others in the village were able to do. So, the stalls which Carris ended up managing were the second-tier type —the flippant kind. The small wins that bring a smile to the face without damaging the purse: the tombola, the coconut shy or the age-old conundrum of guessing the weight of a craftily manufactured cake. Carris had been in charge of the jumble for a few years, and many in the village thought that was where she would stay, but the incident with the lime and green cycling lycra had caused her to think again. Sometimes, the Bring and Buy produce and the British Legion supplies would get muddled, and like most people on the planet, Carris did not want to be reminded of her life's failures. So, this morning, she was pleased to be standing tall with her rodent.

'I thought you spoke beautifully.' Carris said, coming down from the chair she'd been standing on in order to give the rat an extra whoosh as it descended the pipe.

'It seemed to go well.' Julia smiled. Never one to blow her own trumpet.

'The dancing got a bit tangled up.' Carris turned the handmade sign on her trestle table from open to closed.

'Yes.' Julia said, offering Carris a bio-degradable cup full of cold punch from Angie Allworth's apple press. 'They managed to get little Bethany out, eventually.'

Carris' face creased in thought. 'I've never actually seen anyone put the ribbon up their nose and pull it out through their mouth.'

Julia nodded, glancing over at the abandoned maypole with its hacked and mutilated ribbons. 'Apparently, Bethany had been practising for months.'

Carris sighed. 'That girl is very like her mother.'

'The determination of a pit bull.' Julia nodded. Remembering how Bethany's mother, Gemma, had been up all night in the library, reading law books and rehearsing trials. Julia sometimes wondered if the overly legalistic stance of the village might all boil back to Bethany's mum and that genetic determination.

Carris drained the last dregs of punch from her cup before glancing behind her at the chair, the rat and the drainpipe. 'I suppose I'd better get back up. I've made two pounds fifty already, so I'm on a bit of a streak.' She announced proudly.

Julia didn't like to inform the library assistant that for an hour and a half's work, two pounds fifty was not a great deal. It was way below the average minimum wage. They would get more money if they hired Carris out to the local checkouts or a food delivery service. Although maybe that wasn't wise. Carris was numerically challenged and had a notoriously poor sense of direction. 'Here,' Julia said, pulling the chair closer and holding it firm so it didn't sink into the soft grass. 'You just get yourself back up, and I'll hand you all your accoutrements.'

Carris beamed. 'Thank you, Julia. Where would I be without...'

'Don't,' Julia said, a warning in her eyes despite the light tone of her voice. Carris' reprieve was getting all too easy. Every woman should be capable of standing on her own chair and hitting a rat or two if necessary. Dependency could be a bad thing.

As the warm summer sun seeped through Julia's sensible navy Marks and Sparks summer dress, she continued her voyage around the fayre, floating on a little buzz from the fresh apple punch, which Angie insisted had no alcoholic content but, as everyone knew, apples had the propensity to ferment. It was simply in their nature. Julia wasn't sure Angie had the power to stop the process.

Behind her, Julia could hear Carris' delighted tones wafting out over the grass.

'Hit the rat. Hit the rat. Fun for all!'

Julia wasn't convinced that the occupation did, in fact, provide fun for all, although she couldn't help but be secretly impressed by Carris' sales pitch. Perhaps Carris was learning things all the time, gleaning bits of information that she could patch together to make something useful from, like the bunting fluttering from the tea tent. Everything in a village gets used and recycled. Nothing was lost. Perhaps the library would be in safe hands when Julia finally packed up her panniers and left. If Julia could only get the place on a sound financial footing, everything else would fall into place. Like that rat shooting out of the pipe into the swing of the waiting baton, getting everything lined up and ready to roll would be the key.

Julia watched a number of the shows in the big ring as the sun bored down and flakes of hay bale floated across the sky. The husband carrying had always been her favourite event. Most couples ended in a tangled mess, sprawled across the grass, belly laughing, rubbing sore backs and arms and swearing they needed to trim down a bit before another twelve months circled around. There had been years, Julia could remember when this particular event had caused consternation—a bit of husband-swapping going on in order to catch the prize. Taller men with larger player frames were switched in favour of sleeker models—cyclists and runners seemed far more favourable than rugby players or boxers. No one knew if the event was solely responsible for the problem. To many, this seemed a stretch. It was only a "fun" village event, with a sash and a handshake for a prize, and yet marriages had found themselves on the rocks and the men on the scales.

Thankfully, over the last five years or so, the entries have become light-hearted again. Julia had always felt that it does not do to get too competitive over a game. The winner of any game must surely be the person having the most fun. Leaving the crushed bodies behind her, Julia made a further four full swings of the stalls, unable to suppress a smile when she saw that Olivia Dentlow had braved the proceedings.

The young hygienist was standing beside the apple dunking barrel, chatting amicably to Ruth Silverling, who had made a beeline for Olivia on seeing the state of play—Olivia was seven months pregnant. Ruth was revealing herself to be the rag-industry saleswoman that everyone knew her to be, having a rail of styles to suit the blossoming waistline. In turn, Olivia was showing herself for everything that she truly was: a sweet young woman who had been conned. Cruel Benjamin had left her when allegations started to fly with a bun in the oven and her back against the wall. Only now, some months later, was it clear to see that Olivia was an upstanding member of the community, one who needed support, a dress from Ruth Silverling's boutique and a show of solidarity.

In truth, Olivia was exactly the lovely dentist woman that Ben's 20% off code had promised. As for Mr Wiseman, there was no sign. Not even an abandoned coffee cup printed with Ben's logo tumble-weeding in the light wind. As far as the village was concerned, no further evidence was needed—Benjamin Wiseman man was truly the bad egg he'd been suspected of being all along. Even though his specific form of crockery was not the kind Gwyn Thomas had deduced, all was finally well, and as Julia wandered past the happily chatting women, she couldn't help but feel a sense of pride that rationality had prevailed and that, in these modern times, stocks and pillories were only used for fundraising. Wet sponges replaced tomatoes and there was laughter from all. To Julia, on this fine sunny day, it seemed like humanity had come a long way.

All in all, despite the relocation of the fete, the general consensus was that the day had been an overwhelming success. However, on a personal level, you could only admire white elephants, towers of scones, mountains of jumble and dog-eared stacks of donated paperbacks so many times before beginning to feel a little jaded. A position in which Julia soon found herself to be. The buzz of Angie's apple punch had faded, and there had been no sight of Her Ladyship. The conversation that needed to be had remained shelved. The opportunity for such a discussion floated away like the last of the dandelion clocks. Not surprisingly, Julia didn't have the stomach for the hog roast or the cider. The future suddenly seemed vast and uncertain, so she decided to do the only thing a person could do in such a situation—get things just a little more ordered. She nipped into the library and got some admin under her belt. She made sure that she was ready for Monday. She needed peace and quiet and time to think. Besides, the stalls were packing up. The day was done. So, Julia took her bike from where it was parked, unlocked on the edge of the green and cycled leisurely through the quiet streets to the prefab that she often thought of as home.

Julia arrived at the library, and within moments, the lights were on, the alarm was off, and Julia took a seat in front of the computer terminal. She'd decided on her cycle that she would retire sooner than she had planned. Sixty-five didn't seem to be getting any closer, and did it matter? Surely, this was just an arbitrary number. She had a small pension she could draw on and a little savings accruing in her Post Office account. Life, Julia felt, was passing her by, and she didn't want this to happen. There was a new library manager at head office, Mr Perkins, that nobody had met. She wasn't sure that she could cope with the inevitable re-fresh on the reporting front. She had nothing against the man but felt she had used up too many managers over the years.

The stress of the Hortishall books was playing heavily on her mind, and Julia knew that sometimes you just had to let things go. So, her letter of resignation should be addressed to Perkins. Some might feel it was premature. Twelve months were a lot of notice to hand in, but Julia knew it would be best to address the matter upfront before her name was added to the grinding annual wheel of training lists and conferences before more money was invested inadvertently in her learning new systems that she would not be there to implement. Not wanting to let anyone down, she felt twelve months would complete a cycle and give adequate time to get everything under control. She would suggest Carris as her replacement. Carris, she wrote in her letter to Mr Perkins, was well-liked, knew how to repair library books, and could reach the top shelves if standing on a ladder. She was good at selling greeting cards and could, on occasion and if given enough time, be very perceptive. Julia felt it wasn't important to state how she had turned the Hit the Rat stall on its head and had realised that incentives didn't always need to be sweetened. She felt Mr Perkins just wouldn't understand. Carris' fear of the alarm system was certainly a problem, but they had one whole year to work on this, so again, Julia left this off her endorsement.

When the letter was finished, Julia sat back in her flexible office chair, with its articulated backrest and seat creaking harmoniously, feeling an immense sense of satisfaction with her draft. It was a start. Although she would miss the village and the people, she knew that it was time to move on. She would not be staying in Suffolk. It would be difficult, she felt, to go from a position of importance to simply another retiree. Such a transition didn't always work. Besides, she had always fancied living by a crystal blue coast. Wild swimming had become very popular, but Julia didn't want to swim wild anywhere if she couldn't see the bottom. She wanted to keep an eye on her feet, and at five foot six, Julia felt this was a reasonable enough request.

Glancing up from her monitor, she realised with shock that it was already getting dark outside, the evening light leaching from the street, making everything washed out and grey. Luckily, she had lights on her bike and a high-vis tabard. It wouldn't take her long to get home, and the road along the green was well-lit. She gave out one large, satisfied yawn, which smelt disconcertingly of the hotdogs and onions she'd had hours ago at the fete. Vowing to brush her teeth just as soon as she got through her front door, she switched off her terminal, grabbed the broom and was about to hit the alarm when she noticed something strange on the library steps: a strange, crouching outline. It wasn't the welcome sign—she hadn't put that out with the library being closed. It wasn't Geoff. He was fond of sitting on the steps, but with a hog roast and cider on offer at the green, there was not a chance he would have given that up in preference of a little late evening docu-film research.

Cautiously, Julia pulled back the door. Three streets away, she could hear laughter and song from the tail end of the fete, the voices babbling with drink and high spirits, but the street in front of her was eerily quiet.

'Hello?' She called out into the narrow, grey road which seemed to envelop her, but there was no reply.

Glancing down at the top step, she saw that the object sitting there was a cardboard box. It seemed strange. It was an odd time for a delivery when the library was closed. Bending to lift the box, Julia was surprised by its weight. The thing weighed more than a child-size sack of potatoes. Could it be potatoes? This didn't seem logical. Bending her knees and angling her arms like a forklift truck, just as she had been told to do during her library management training on lifting, Julia firmly grabbed and manoeuvred the box to the front desk. Yet something at the back of Julia's brain would not sit still, an uncomfortable niggle that all was not right.

She had been in the library. Whoever dropped the box off must have seen this, so why didn't they come in? Nothing about it made sense. Cautiously, she lifted one flap on the corner of the box and peered in.

'Bernard.' She said, expelling the name in a huff. Bernard had been managing the bookstall, and this was just his style—dumping all his unsold tat back on the library. She glanced at the covers. These were cheap paperbacks, damp and dusty. Inside the covers, someone had scribbled in pencil "60 pence" or "ten for a pound." They were useless. Although Julia had to say it, these kinds of books were the sort best for burning, and burning or pulping old books was a thing which broke the poor library manager's heart. Sadly, she would have to go through them all, one by one, just in case there were any gems in the dross.

Suddenly, a clatter outside in the street made her jump. *Bernard*, she thought, her face composed itself into a frown. He was at it again. She rushed to the door, ready to call him out and make him haul the books home. Yet again, the street was empty, but sitting on the library steps were four more boxes. Each one was as big and fat as the last. Julia's face furrowed into a heavy frown. Something about this was not stacking up. Bernard had a bad back. How could a man of eighty-five be dumping all these heavy boxes on her door and then scarpering off double-quick into the cover of dusk?

Standing on the top step as the early summer evening air chilled around her, Julia opened another box, and her heart sank. Sitting atop the pulp fiction paperbacks, glaring up at her in brilliant white, was a letter. It was addressed "To Whom It May Concern." Her heart sinking, Julia took the envelope gently into her hands and slowly turned it over. Instantly, her suspicions were confirmed—it was sealed with the Hortishall crest.

7

THE HALL

Julia stood beneath the wary eyes of the twin stone eagles as they peered down on her from their high perch, a look of scorn on their granite-hard faces. She didn't care; her own attention was focused elsewhere—towards the house. It was still early, well before nine. Somewhere across the Hall's sprawling lawns, possibly at the edge of the wooded area that led to the stone, sunken garden, Julia could hear the flute-like tones of a blackbird calling in the day. Yet despite the birdsong and the soft blue summer light ebbing through the low trails of morning mist, the many-eyed monster of the Hall remained sleeping. Its windows, although un-curtained, stared out towards the grounds, blank and indifferent. Not one sign of life could be seen beyond those tall iron gates. Her Ladyship's racing green Mercedes squatted on the gravel driveway in the exact same position it had been *squatting* in for over a month. Its fat tyres sank like satisfied farts into the deep gravel. Julia doubted the car had moved since His Lordship breathed his last. This, however, did not mean that Her Ladyship was at home. Lady Hortishall was a woman who loved to be on the move, to shake things up. It was a well-known fact in the county that Her Ladyship was faster with her graphite black credit card than a quick-draw cowboy. The woman also had an aversion to carrying the multitude of tastefully logoed, reinforced boutique bounty bags that she'd happily accrue on any of her frequent jaunts to the neighbouring towns. Therefore, she often resorted to a little pre-paid muscle provided by a hired driver.

No, the presence of Lady Hortishall's car did not mean Her Ladyship was at home. For all Julia knew, Lady Hortishall could have dumped the books on the library steps the previous evening, then sped off in some chauffeured vehicle towards the airport and Monaco. Apparently, Monaco was packed to the brim with rich people wanting to escape more than just the late fees on their library books.

Unlike the abandoned Mercedes, Reece's peacock-blue Lexus was, however, no longer present. Julia had noticed that Reece hadn't been up at the Hall for over a week. It would seem that the business of dying had been done. All apart from the delivery of Julia's books. But was Reece aware of that particular situation? It seemed unlikely that he would have been included in the murky details—Her Ladyship's cunning revision with the terms of the will substituting a junkyard of pulp fiction titles for the rare antiquities collected lovingly over decades by the Hall's more literate owners. Reece and Her Ladyship were not, after all, on social terms. No doubt the solicitor would have reminded the "grieving" but dry-eyed widow that the books were owed, but he would not have overstepped his position as an advisor. She wasn't a child, and Reece was a man who knew all too well on which side his bread wore its honey. Julia imagined that Her Ladyship would have dismissed the issue of the promised books with a few casual words and a vague flick of her pin-thin, gold braceleted arms. An indeterminate dismissal could have implied that the matter had been dealt with, and Reece would have, in good conscience, been thankful to let the matter drop.

However, the situation had changed. Her Ladyship was playing fast and loose with the truth, and action needed to be taken. Julia took comfort in the fact that there did not appear to be any security cameras on the gate and felt surprisingly appreciative of the leylandii hedge, which, as was only in its nature, was now providing excellent coverage. Although she had to admit that she didn't enjoy skulking around on the front line. It was not her style, and she had certainly felt braver only a few short hours ago.

IT HAD BEEN easy to feel heroic from the comfort of her small two-up, two-down terrace at the edge of the village—the rented home she had been in since she first arrived at the small rural community over thirty years ago. She had decided resolutely, over her English Breakfast tea and a single slice of granary toast, with its thin smear of butter and hint of honey, that she should pay Her Ladyship a visit. They needed to talk.

This decision had not come to Julia on a whim. No, she had been up most of the night in the community library, bent over the damp boxes of books, a sense of weariness laying heavy on her heart. She wouldn't have wanted to admit it to the wider public, and all that goes on in a library (when the doors were closed and the lights were dim) remained as sacrosanct as the information gleaned in a confessional due to the non-disclosure compliances all librarians were expected to sign. However, as Julia had flopped each damp, unwanted title onto the honeyed veneer desk in front of her, she had felt a genuine stab of pain at their condition. The pages of the volumes were stuck together. Rotted by the passage of time and one too many disastrous car-boot sales, occasions when the weather had turned, and a tarpaulin was not to hand. Slowly, over the years, the pages of the books had festered. From a brilliant cream with a dry sawdust smell and a hearty swish, when flicked with the thumb to a moulded, indifferent grey block. Julia was not a woman for emotion, and yet that night, a single tear had slid down the library manager's high-coloured cheek as she read through the dusty, damaged titles. It seemed to Julia that this must surely be the final evidence that the mighty had fallen. By *mighty,* she was thinking—the literati, herself and the manor—Hortishall Hall had been known for its serious literature. Volumes were collected over decades by the shy but voracious reader, Eloise.

The books in cardboard boxes, dumped in true hit-and-run style, and currently moulding on Julia's desk did not fit Eloise's reading profile: *Aliens versus Garden Gnomes—the Epic Showdown*. This might have interested the gardening club (at a push), but Julia couldn't imagine it would have been something that the young Eloise Hortishall would have held dear. Even leaving the fiction to one side, as fiction readers were often fickle, *The Quantum Banana Paradox* by Dr Fuzzbutt Nebulon had very little hard science behind it.

There was, of course, only one fact that could be gleaned from any of the books so hastily delivered to Julia's door—Lady Hortishall was attempting to circumnavigate the donation that had been promised. The tsunami of pulp abandoned in the darkening village after the British Legion Fete was winding down and morphing into something quite different, involving cider, loud, raucous whoops, and the forced falsetto tones of Salvatori—the rurally stranded opera singer was always keen to give vent to his pipes when his wife's organ was not belting out a tune. The timing of the book delivery had indeed been tactical; it was intended to slow down and finally silence Julia's legitimate requests.

~

YET NOW, the very next morning, all was quiet. The manor appeared to be sleeping innocently under the first bloom of the day. The gates were closed, and the eagles were watching. Julia did, however, notice something new: a freshly painted sign hanging upon the brickwork read "No Callers." It could seem a tad superfluous; it was clear from the bared gates that nobody was getting in unless invited. However, the additional sign felt curiously like a hard punch to the solar plexus. Julia felt her world slipping away. The fearlessness she had felt when holding a slice of granary in her hand, as the kettle sang on the Aga, and her bicycle waited patiently outside the white-painted fence for her day to begin, all that gallantry had gone.

Julia had no way of getting through the gates to talk to Her Ladyship, and without the gift of Lord Hortishall's books, the library manager felt certain that her own small, imperfect but treasured, rural bibliotheca would struggle to establish its future. The building was in dire need of repairs, and since the pandemic had left funding depleted, the council could no longer be expected to cough up. There were only so many pens, pencils and gift cards that a rural establishment could sell. Julia had argued many times, at many management meetings, that putting up the over-due fines was not an option. This only ever served to deter readers from borrowing. This continual mental carousel of doom and gloom was why Julia's heart felt so very heavy on such a fine, clear morning. Handing the library on to Carris without the expected influx of the Hortishall books would be like offering the woman a spaceship on the approach of a gargantuan meteor but omitting to give her the keys.

As Julia watched the house, pained by her inability to take action, her gaze scanned wistfully over the grounds of the Hall. Conjuring up happier times when Beatrice Bell's organs ran clear, and a settled future seemed secured. Despite such glorious weather fresh for the day and the beauty of the sprawling Elizabethan manor, Julia couldn't help but feel irked. She couldn't help but wonder at the injustice of having one very small, thin and badly read woman living all alone in so many rooms (one of which happened to be a library).

She was about to turn and remount her bike, girding her mind for the morning ahead. There was surely nothing that could be done here when suddenly a shaft of sunlight broke from the sky, picking out a small square of the driveway, the patch which happened to contain a majestic cedar. The tree that had stood beside the Hall for as long as anyone could remember. A beautiful specimen, much admired by dendrologists up and down the country. Its wide, open, eternal grace seemed to give the library manager a little peace. *Time*, it seemed to say, *will ease out the wrinkles of the small-minded, of the petty, of the unjust.* However, just as Julia was taking a little pleasure in those wide sweeping branches and the mantra circling her head, she realised there was something badly wrong. Illuminated in the glow of the wide arc-light sunbeam, balancing on a single, precariously extended arm of the tree, was Curtis' cat.

People said the ginger tom was Curtis' cat, but in truth, Curtis, the Hortishall's long-time gardener and handyman, had never owned it. He had found the poor, sad creature one autumn under a heap of mouldering leaves. The thing was barely alive. There wasn't enough breath left in its sad lungs to give even the smallest of mews. Now, Curtis was not known for his kindness. Countrymen often had attitudes which could appear cold to the wider world. Living so close to the seasons, they appeared to develop an innate awareness of natural selection—a propensity to not interfere. This could seem out of sync with the modern world. Countrymen were often accused of being cold. This misapprehension, Julia had always felt, was due to the bearded nature of such men. It was almost impossible to tell when they were smiling benignly, an attitude which Curtis must have been wearing that autumn when he discovered the cat since he had lovingly nursed the frail tabby back to life.

Over the next ten years, Curtis' decision to save the cat may have been something he regretted. The ginger tom may have doted on the bearded, mono-syllabic Curtis, but the small thing seemed to be a bundle of big trouble, and it had proceeded to place Curtis in many testing predicaments. One year, it got isolated on an ice flow, a situation which could have ended in tragedy for all. Another year, it sauntered into the road and caused mayhem with an underage driver. Every other week, it seemed as though it got itself hijacked by a delivery van or builder, winding up all over the country. Curtis constantly had to put the cat basket on his motorbike, don his leathers and ride off to the far reaches of the kingdom in order to retrieve the catastrophic feline. The gardener (notwithstanding the beard), never one for smiles and bonhomie, had nevertheless done his duty by the thing.

Only now, on this fine, quiet morning, the poor ginger tabby was stuck high in the wide arms of the cedar, and Curtis was nowhere to be seen. The cat's mournful mew carried on the damp morning air seemed desperate and afraid. The cat was getting old. Of late, its body had become so thin that if you picked the thing up, it felt as though you were holding nothing but a handful of bones. Calling the thing seventeen years would have been too kind. It was twenty if it was a day, and everyone in the town knew it was only a matter of time before the prankster situations the animal seemed inclined to get itself into would one day prove too much.

The village was also painfully aware that when the time came, Curtis, despite his beard, would be broken. For the past six months, the Women's Institute had been scanning the classified ads for a litter of ginger kittens. One of which might help ease the pain of an ageing countryman's heart. As Julia watched the impending catastrophe anxiously from beyond the gates, her mind sped through a million ghastly consequences. Why, she wondered, did this have to happen on her watch? Beyond the gate, across the driveway, and up in the tree, the bag-of-bones fluff-ball of a cat mewed plaintively. Julia's heart got stuck in her throat as, cautiously, the cat stuck out one thin, stripped paw out in front, wobbling just a little more than was truly safe. The tree was high. A fall from those branches would mean certain death.

Julia pressed her face a little closer to the iron railings, desperately attempting to ascertain the presence of Curtis. If not the man himself, then perhaps a sign—his wheelbarrow or his sit-on mower with its perky but highly toxic puffs of diesel. Black gusts always clouded behind him in the mower's wake. But no, the air was as clean as a whisper, and Curtis' rusted barrow with its wonky wheel and high-pitched, lopping squeal was nowhere to be seen. The man could be anywhere; the grounds were abominably vast. Meanwhile, the old and withered ginger cat mewed pitifully from the wide horizontal layers of the tree. Another paw was tentatively struck beyond the small body. The branch bowed. Julia knew she had to act. The job had fallen on her ample shoulders, and the library manager had never been the type to shirk responsibility.

Luckily, there was a gap between the leylandii and the stone pillars of the eagles. A gap wide enough to allow the passage of one rather large library manager. Without another thought for her own personal safety, Julia pushed her bulk through. The cat would not die on Julia's watch.

~

EVERYBODY KNEW it was illegal to use a phone when riding a bike, but Potter's Descent was a road rarely travelled, and besides, this was an emergency. The cat might be safe, but Julia's trouble seemed to be just beginning.

'Carris?' Julia shouted into her handset, conversing with Carris' answerphone, as the cool morning air sped past Julia's flushed face, nipping at her cheeks and tearing at her curls. 'I'm going to be late. You need to open up.' Julia waited for a moment, wondering if there was anything more that she should add. She wondered, whilst the speed of the bike increased since she was unable to manage the brakes and the phone at the same time, was that enough? Should she have said something more? The wheels whirred faster, as did the cogs in Julia's brain. Yes, yes, of course, Julia had missed something—something of vital importance. 'You *can* do this, Carris.' She added, hoping against hope that this was, in fact, true.

'REECE,' Julia said, with the sound of her banging on the solicitor's door still ringing in her ears. 'We need to talk,' her wide lips spluttered into the silence of the hallway.

Reece was standing inside the passageway. It was a narrow corridor running the width of the Old Yarn Woollen Shop situated next door. It was a simple affair with an entrance cubicle to Reece's place of work, which permanently smelt of wet paint and junk mail. Yet, nobody could remember the last time that the place had been granted a lick of anything fresh. Normally, this would not have mattered, not one jot, because this vestibule wasn't the sort of place that one would stop in for a conversation. There simply wasn't the room. It led, in three short strides, to a narrow flight of stairs which climbed their way precariously towards the legal offices of Reece Trumpington and Son. Reece did not actually have a son or, for that matter, a romantic life partner, but the "son" had been on the signage when he had taken over the office many years ago. The young Reece had asked for Artie Tintwell (who did all the signs in the village and was just starting out himself) for the writing on Reece's new sign to be in exactly the same clear, crisp, golden font as the "son" inscribed on the old sign. Due to a misunderstanding on Artie's part, the "son" itself had been carried over. Reece would have removed it but had always suffered from a terrible case of imposter syndrome mixed with a heavy spoonful of superstition. As everyone knew, it was unlucky to go about changing names. Do it once, and you may have gotten away with it—twice, and you were asking for trouble. Besides, Reece felt the "son" gave his business a subliminal sense of legacy and permanence, which people might trust. He was only just out of law school when he took on the office. Therefore, any kind of legitimacy he could shoe-horn himself into, he was keen to adopt. The "son" had stuck.

If Reece was disappointed that the promised child had never materialised, he certainly never mentioned it, and after a while, people simply forgot about the missing "son". Instead, Reece enjoyed the stability and respect from the village that a respected father figure might well enjoy. In turn, he liked his life, with his large empty house and his peacock-blue car in peace. He was always keen to get to his office each morning and wallow in a sense of peace and permanence before the day began.

Only this morning, he hadn't even made it up the stairs. Normally, a person would ring the bell in the street outside and Marsha Wallace, Reece's long-time help and hindrance, would buzz them in. Marsha was a moaner. She was always late and always in an unspecified pain of some sort and permanently disgruntled, but more than happy to press the entrance buzzer from her desk, situated at the top of the steep, narrow steps and through the crinkled glass-panelled door. Marsha liked to let those seeking justice in. Nobody was ever supposed to meet in the hallway. Reece maintained (rather monotonously, if truth be told) that there was a place for everything, and everything had a place. The hallway was only ever a place of transition, and yet here was Julia blustering in behind him on this fine morning. She barely gave Reece the chance to remove his coat, drop his keys back into his case, or adopt his usual wisdom-of-Solomon demeanour.

Reece was a man who didn't like to be put out of his routine. His leathery, long face, tanned to perfection on the golf courses of the Algarve, palled momentarily at the interruption. 'Julia?' He said, clearly disturbed by the sight of the dishevelled library manager, a woman known for her sound sense of appropriate style and exemplary posture. 'Are you alright?' His face crumpled into a crisscross of a frown. 'Take a minute.' He instructed and took himself a long, low breath, as though demonstrating the appropriate response in situations of extreme panic and injustice. At this point in time, Reece could not have known the exact reason for the panic and injustice, but he would have known instinctively that panic and injustice were present. After all, this was the very nature of his business. 'Breathe,' he said, illustrating the instruction and going possibly one step further than necessary. Being a man of authority and the law, Reece had discovered that people liked nothing more than clear instructions.

'Oh, Reece. I have such terrible news.' Julia blustered, unable to look the solicitor in the eye, her sense of foolishness being so acute. Someone was trying to pull the wool over her eyes, and she wasn't thinking about the yarn from the shop next door. Her heavy heart was still banging against her ribs from her frantic hillside descent. She was flushed, feeling fraught, foolish and frantic. Quite frankly—a good deal of the "f" emotions rolled into a snowball of boundless buzzing energy. In truth, at the very core of all this agitation, Julia was feeling that she had failed—failed Carris, the village and the library system as a whole, and perhaps even her life's mission. For who knew what their life's mission was until they got to the end? The jury was still out, and it had certainly not been saving the cat. Small triumphs aside, Julia couldn't help feeling that being duped on the books had been a foolishness she should not have been made to bear. In short, for a big woman, Julia was suddenly feeling decidedly small. 'The books...' she blurted, finally raising her gaze and staring straight into Reece's green watery eyes. 'Lord Hortishall's bequeathed books. They're gone.'

~

REECE HAD DECIDED, in his wisdom as community solicitor and possibly because his secretary, Marsha, did not arrive till ten, that Julia needed a coffee *tout de suite*. Therefore, they should relocate to Sal's Snippy Biscuit. Thankfully, the village Primary School of St Martin's in the Meadows was on its annual day trip to Freddy's Farm, so the usual proliferation of exhausted mothers, tiny tots, sticky fingers, and visible tonsils was not present. The flustered mothers would be otherwise engaged, dressed in fluorescent tabards, counting bobbing heads and dolling out duck food.

The café was quiet, and Sal was all too happy to set two mugs of steaming hot coffee down on the pot-ringed table in front of her guests.

'Start from the beginning, Julia.' Reece said, adding to the coffee the sweeteners he always carried with him in the hidden top pocket of his silky-smooth blue jacket.

Without being told, Julia took a deep breath, wondering as the coffee and cinnamon-scented air flitted through her lungs where exactly the beginning happened to sit. In truth, she wasn't at all clear. 'It's about the will.' She decided, realising that this was, in fact, what the entire problem boiled down to. 'The promised books.'

Julia felt a tinge of disappointment when she noted the small but perceptible sag of Reece's shoulders. He refrained from rolling his eyes, but Julia got the distinct impression that if he didn't have a reputation as an upstanding member of the community who had a truly model son, a large house with its mortgage paid off, and in the fortunate position of knowing where all the village's unwanted "bodies" were buried (metaphorically speaking), he would have rolled his eyes. Luckily, being a person acutely aware that you only get to be in a position such as the above by a steadfast control of personal mannerisms, the eye roll remained undone.

'I did ask Her Ladyship,' Reece let slip a small sigh, taking a moment to run one leathery, walnut hand through his greying hair. 'I'm sure that the books will be arriving soon.'

Before the words could even squeeze themselves out of her mouth, Julia's head was shaking defensively. 'That's the problem, Reece. Well, not the main problem, at least.' Julia gazed down into the dark reaches of her mochaccino with its splash of Kenyan Roost, which should, of course, be "Kenyan Roast." But Artie had taken over chalking up Sal's board with her special blends, and Artie's decidedly quirky way with words meant that the coffees never quite appeared as intended anymore. 'I did take a delivery of books last night.' Julia said, drawing out her words as though there was a lot more weight packed beneath each utterance than simply that of transferring a literal meaning.

'Well,' Reece smiled, sitting back in his chair. His shoulders sank into their habitual coat-hanger straight line, and a genuine smile brightened his face. 'Problem over.'

'No, Reece.' Julia shook her head slowly. 'It feels to me as though the problem is just beginning. I received five boxes of books last night.'

'So,' Reece raised his large hands in a gesture which was supposed to be reassuringly dismissive. 'I'm sure the rest will be on their way. They would have taken up a lot of room in the car, and Her Ladyship is over eighty.'

'The car hasn't moved,' Julia said and promptly wished she'd left this bit out. It sounded as though she had been stalking Lady Hortishall. 'I cycle past each morning.' She said in a matter-of-fact manner, filling the awkward gap that had wedged itself into the conversation with a little bantered bluster. 'But, Reece, we're getting off point here. It's not about transportation. These were not...' and she halted abruptly, realising just in time that she was about to say "not *my* books." She realised that this would have added a proprietorial bias, which simply should not have been there. Julia took another deep breath. 'These were not the right books. The books that arrived last night were cheap paperbacks, the kind you can pick up in bulk from a charity shop.'

Reece looked confused. 'Well, nothing can account for taste,' he said diplomatically. 'It's not for me to judge the reading habits of others.'

It certainly wasn't for Reece to judge. Julia knew the man's reading material inside out, and he was the last person to be throwing stones. However, he was getting off track.

'They weren't the right books, Reece.' Julia felt her voice rising in a note of panic. 'Her Ladyship is trying to fob us off.'

'But Julia...' Reece sounded serious, carrying all the gravitas of a solicitor's tone as it was possible to get behind two single words. 'How do you know what Lord Hortishall had in his library?'

For the second occasion that morning, Julia felt her world plummet. In order to know the contents of the library, she would have to admit that she had been in the room. Not only that, she would be forced to confess that she had perused the shelves and taken herself a little impromptu inventory.

Time seemed to slow, the world revolved in wider, more ponderous loops than its regular trajectory as Julia's mind whirled through a plethora of explanations, scenarios and situations which might, conceivably, if hinted and squinted at, have some semblance of an acceptable truth. Her pink lips dropped open, readying a response that her brain was still uncertain of. She had been caught out. She was guilty of some crime. Of what, she was unsure, but whatever misdemeanour it was, there was only one thing for certain—it would be headlines in the local newspaper. Sal was listening, and the coffee shop owner was on very good terms with Gareth from the Gazette. He'd grown weary lately of retired butcher stories taking up the headlines, or is growing the biggest pumpkin or the height of Mimsy Davenport's dahlias. Cuttings of every kind of prize plant were always shared around the village, so the horticultural elements held no great story impact from year to year. Gareth was after fresh meat, not involving butchery, and Julia could well provide it. Everyone's perception of the honest, caring woman she surely was would be cracked down the middle. Vomited from the collective consciousness causing a Sea Change of hostility, she couldn't let this happen.

Luckily, she suddenly found herself in the fortunate position of not offering a reply. There was a clatter of feet on the steps outside the café. The crack of a terracotta pot as somebody lumbered thoughtlessly past, and the door to the small café on the green banged open with an unnatural force. The bell jarred, jittering on its wire like a demented budgerigar. Ringing out manically into the still morning air of the shop, the flapping door finally came to a halt, revealing the old, dishevelled Silas Mariner. His face was agape in horror. His eyes were wild. His entire body shaking like a pneumatic drill. 'She's done it.' He blurted. 'She's actually done it.'

Reece and Julia turned in their seats towards the door

and Silas. Behind them, Sal stopped crafting a foam heart on the top of a latte. All mouths stopped as the cappuccino machine vomited out dark liquid with nothing beneath it to catch the dark gold. All eyes watched. A sense of dread lay so heavily in the air you could cut it up in slices and serve it instead of snacks at the next Bring and Buy.

'That Lady Hortishall.' Silas muttered in a true deranged fashion. Inserting a pronoun, which, although not strictly necessary, Julia found herself admiring. 'She's dropped her bombshell.'

8

THE FINAL STRAW

In the pub, later that evening, the "bombshell" found itself strapped into a variety of different headings. "Unleashing the bombshell" was perhaps the favourite. Although many felt this didn't do it justice, arguing that it was important to be more specific—emphasise the devastating effect of the metaphorical weaponry which had indeed been *unleashed*. Marsha, Reece's secretary, felt "nuked us now" worked well. Julia noticed that Gareth from the Gazette scribbled the strapline down in his notebook. He was the sort of journalist who survives principally on alliterative powers and wry headlines rather than any accurate or insightful portrayal of facts. Julia also noted that Reece gave Gareth a surreptitious but withering look before reminding Marsha (loudly) that their law firm did have affiliations with the Hortishall Estate, and "nuke" might be seen as an inflammatory term. Silas said it couldn't be thought of in any other way. Being a man with a penchant for arson, Silas was most probably the expert on the matter. Unfortunately, the conversation looked in danger of veering off in totally the wrong direction, and nobody in the village could afford for it to do that, because according to Lady Hortishall's last communication, which had been hammered on the noticeboard in the Post Office as well as stuck on posts around the common's perimeter—the common was not so common after all. She wanted them all off and was giving them the required legal notice.

Whilst the hubbub grew louder, Gareth, looking decidedly shifty, put down his pen, and Julia wondered how far the journalist was embedded into the Hortishall payroll system. He enjoyed calling the folks at the Hall "The Honourable Hortishalls," even though they had not received any honours since the seventeenth century. It was also a curious fact that Gareth had not written one bad word about the Hall's owners, not even about the leylandii incident. In fact, as it turned out, many people were in hock to the Hortishalls, not least Curtis, having gardened at the Hall for more years than he cared to remember. It crossed Julia's mind that the debate might be stacked and that having an unbiased conversation could prove problematic. However, being on the payroll didn't mean that you had sold your soul. Thankfully, when Curtis had been asked his views on the Lady Hortishall *bombshell* matter and what they should call it, he had grunted sagely before offering up a simple but curiously satisfying prophet of doom style delivery: 'She's done it now.'

Curtis could be forgiven for the short, terse reply. His mind was elsewhere, for tucked inside the buttons of the man's overlarge beer-brown waxed jacket was the poor ginger tabby. Its head poked out of Curtis' collar for the occasional quick check-in to the proceedings before disappearing once again into the ample folds of Curtis' coat. Earlier that morning, Julia had managed to get the creature safely out of the cedar and wrapped it gently in her coat for the gardener to find and feed. It would appear that now Curtis was taking no chances on the luckless tabby. On hearing Lady Hortishall's *done it now* news, the long-time gardener and handyman had promptly handed in his notice. He had taken the cat from the shed where Julia had left it safe and warm, lifting the warm bundle of ginger fur into his wide arms. Life for Curtis and the tabby suddenly seemed far too short. The clock was ticking. The world was there to be enjoyed, to squeeze the last drops of sunshine from because Curtis knew that no amount of substitute tabbies could ease the pain when that inevitable day finally arrived.

However, not everyone was taking the high ground on the latest Hortishall issue or willing to leave it to fate to administer a much-needed dollop of karma. Many wanted to call the latest run-in with the estate "the final straw." This seemed to conjure up seductive revolutionary vibes. It was wondered if they should count the pitchforks in the village —wondered, until PC Mumblings reminded the gathered that pitchforks could be construed as a weapon, and what good would it do the village if everyone got arrested? There would be no one to walk on the common, let alone look at the damn thing.

Mark Tanner came up with "over my dead body," which didn't have the same call to action as "the final straw," implying a less direct response and way more personal sacrifice. It was a bit Ghandi-like. Besides, the dead body part was a sore subject. Mark's days of action were long gone. His hedge had been pulled down, and his nude modelling workshops had been abandoned. At one hundred and seven, everyone knew that Mark's cancer was finally catching up with him. He wasn't shy about the fact, frankly admitting it every time he was given the chance to open his mouth. He had even started his own crowdfunding page on CashSplash, inviting donations—so he could get to Dignitas and be out of this sorry mess of a world where everyone was forced to wear shoes—his exact words. So far, he hadn't scraped up enough to get himself to Dover. Therefore, Mark's offering of his body to step across did nothing but remind those gathered in the Dog and Duck of their own mortality, as well as made them uncomfortably aware that they really should have put a fiver into his fund. In short, Mark's contribution had always detracted from the situation at hand; the action needed to address Her Ladyship's last bombshell.

Gemma, who was studying the law, had taken it upon herself to head the impromptu meeting in the ladies' bar. Unlike Reece, Gemma was an impartial advisor—not on the Hortishall payroll. Such was Gemma's dedication to the particular matter that she had even brought little Bethany along, even though it was well past the child's bedtime. The landlord, Regi Brewhound, had made an exception to the no-children rule enforced at the Dog and Duck—these were unprecedented circumstances.

Not everyone was happy. Rules were supposedly there for a reason. Prue Purlington, who owned the Old Yarn, looked decidedly on edge at the child's presence. Expecting a long night, Prue had arrived with her sewing bag packed to the brim with freshly wound, butter-soft skeins of Merino. Considering what Bethany had done at the British Legion Fete with ribbons from the maypole and most of the available orifices on her face, Prue was understandably wary. Nobody wants to be wearing a designer jumper that's had its strands pulled up the nose and through the wide open mouth of a youngster. However, everyone was glad that Gemma was there to advise on the legal aspects and legitimacy of the matter. So, nobody brought Bethany up.

'It does seem unfair,' Gemma said, her arms held out towards the gathered like Moses as she attempted to stem the tide of vitriol. 'The common is owned by the Hortishall estate, but it's been used as common land since the fifteenth century.'

'Exactly,' Eddy Bright from the Parish Council chirped up.

Eddy's decisive affirmation invited a general chorusing from the locals. The usual things, 'yes,' 'absolutely' and 'well said,' as though they had all been present since the fifteenth century and knew all about it.

'Only…' Gemma's previous confidence seemed to crack as she reached behind herself for a fat wedge of documents propped up on the mahogany-glazed table beside Bethany. 'By some omission, the common was not registered in the 1965 Commons Registration Act.'

A low, dissatisfied murmur passed around the Dog and Duck. Several hostile pairs of eyes shot in Eddy's direction. Although it was hardly his fault. He would have been around four years old at the time. Luckily, Gemma, as always, had a few hints as to the oversight.

'Possibly because…' Gemma said, flitting her eyes over a single document, reading the bold type at speed, 'it was a kind of permissive arrangement.'

'Permissive?' Ruth Silverling's plump, pretty face crumpled under the word. Ruth was the sort of woman that everyone avoided having on their team when buddying up for Scrabble. She'd also crawled out of the same schooling system as Carris.

'In this case,' Gemma said, taking a deep breath, '*permis-*

sive means that the Hortishall estate owns the common but allows the community usage.'

Reece cleared his throat, leaning forward eagerly in his chair in order to offer a healthy dose of mansplaining. 'The key thing here is that permissive *allows* the usage. It is not obligatory.'

Ruth Silverling let out a tiny, bright laugh. 'Well, of course not. I wouldn't want anyone having to make me walk on the common. I don't need to anyway,' she said with a simple shrug. 'My figure is just the way I like it. Exercise not needed,' she said with an assurance most in the room envied, although many thought it was misplaced. 'Besides, I access my shop over the green.'

There were a couple of nods over this. The green was, after all, safe. That triangle of land was not in dispute. It would appear that only the common had a misnomer attached.

'But I can't get into my cottage,' Silas shouted, his eyes wild. 'If there's no access over the common, I'm cut off.'

'Or trapped in,' Ruth offered, trying but failing to be helpful.

It wasn't just Silas that would have the problem. Annexing off the common would inconvenience many in the community. To Julia, it simply didn't seem right.

'I don't understand,' she said thoughtfully. 'Surely, since the common has been used since the fifteenth century, we have rights of access.'

Gemma took in a deep breath. 'Well, yes, but sadly in this case...' She paused, trying to collect her words and make sense of a situation which could easily take five hundred lawyers and as many years to unravel. 'You see, there's a clause in the deeds to the estate about the Hall and the common.'

If Gemma had been for a response, she would have been disappointed. By now, the entire gathering in the pub had adopted an eerie silence. Reluctantly, she pulled a deep breath out of the silent air. 'It's because the green was recently separated from the common.'

A look of confusion passed around the gathered.

'Not true.' Silas piped up. 'My eyesight might be going, but I would have noticed if someone had been out there building a wall.'

There was a lot of backslapping at this point. A couple of indignant 'what does the woman take us for?' type of comments delivered in the local hard, burly accent and a smattering of much relished hard-core swearing. The colourful language caused Prue to offer some off-cuts of Merino to Bethany hoping that the child might stuff something up her ears.

'It was at the Royal British Legion.' Gemma said, raising her voice to cut through the chatter. 'The fete.'

This caused a titter of laughter to circulate—how could the fete have closed the common off from the green? The thought was daft. The common was as wide as a small sea.

'We were all there.' Megan Keeble offered lightly. 'I think we would have noticed.' She laughed. So did the others, but Julia couldn't help noticing—Gemma was not laughing.

'It was the hay bales.' Gemma said, barely audible.

'Sorry, sorry.' Des said loudly. 'Could we all just...sorry, but I can't hear.'

The din began to subside, all eyes returning to Gemma.

'The hay bales,' she said sadly. 'The ones that we'd put out to stop people from wandering away. We all did it.' Gemma eyed the gathered village with an all-inclusive sadness. 'Every one of us. We gave our common away.'

FOR MORE THAN A WEEK, the village encountered what Arthur Miller might have described as "a bit of a witch hunt." It was true that each and every member of the small rural community had pulled themselves up a hay bale and sat on it to eat a slice of cake, watch a little dancing, or gossip about Bethany's amazing trick with her nose and her mouth. Wondering from the comfort of their seat, had it been worth the cost of the ribbons hacked from the maypole? In truth, the village had been thankful for the place to rest, never thinking for a moment that it would be turned so bitterly against them. It made the insult of Lady Hortishall reclaiming the common cut just that little bit deeper since they had all been unwittingly complicit.

But the thing that really caused rancour was of a slightly different nature—how did Her Ladyship know about the wall of hay? She hadn't been to the event. Gareth checked diligently through all the photos that the Gazette had posted on the website and in the paper itself, and not one image showed the treacherous hay wall. Twitter, Facebook and My Book were all trawled through, looking for an unwitting snap which could have caused such a seismic upheaval. Naturally, they suspected Reece due to his close affiliation to the Hall, but the poor man swore on his bible that he didn't babble. Curtis was easily let off the hook. He said he had only ever been on grunting terms with Her Ladyship. She ordered, and he grunted. It had worked for years. Going by his communications with the rest of the village, there seemed no necessity to doubt that Curtis was telling the truth.

The only comfort to be gleaned from the trauma was that the mystery of the mole and the loss of the common had pushed Julia's own concerns over the missing books out of the picture. The entire village was currently under threat. People started proposing all kinds of ingenious and, quite frankly, problematic solutions designed to secure access to all tithe cottages.

St Martin's in the Meadows Primary School had even designed an architectural competition judged by Silas. The entire classes of years four, five and six sharpened their pencils and opened their minds. The design which Silas eventually favoured featured a slide. However, as was the case with any architectural initiatives designed by the under tens, there were problems. The slide, although it looked good on paper, had a core fault in its application. Although it was brilliantly fast and efficient at transporting Silas from his cottage, there was a logistical problem in getting him back in. The images were unveiled in the village hall, and the first, second and third awards were handed out, but after the medals were given, a disappointment settled back upon the shoulders of the adults. The slide would not truly work.

Besides, the problem was not just about accessing the cottages. The problem was the terrible sense of betrayal. Lady Hortishall had diddled them, and what was even worse, there was a mole in the village. Someone who had sneaked the information about the hay bales to the Hall. Someone who must have known about the laws over the common land. Someone who could profit from disclosing such a situation to Her Ladyship.

'It makes you distrust everyone.' Artie Winston said, chalking up Sal's sign in the café the very day after the architectural awards had been doled out.

Carris found herself quivering at the horror of a world in which everyone had to be looking over their shoulders and watching their backs. 'I don't like to think about it.'

'Me neither.' Ruth Silverling happened to be in there, grabbing a coffee for a client who was having a tricky fitting. The woman swore she was a size ten, but as Ruth had told the coffee shop when she entered in search of caffeinated libation, the woman was clearly a sixteen from the waist down. 'Do you think it could be Mark?'

In truth, Ruth had never been fond of Mark. They both saw the world so differently. Ruth simply couldn't understand the attraction of naturism when there were so many gorgeous fabrics to drape across the body.

'There's no way it was Mark who spilt the beans,' Julia said, nipping the matter in the bud. The man didn't own a car or a phone, so unless he was sending post by pigeons up to the Hall, Julia couldn't see how he could seriously be considered as an informant.

Unsurprisingly, Ruth did not want to let go of her prime suspect. She did have a bit of an axe to grind—Mark had never spent a penny in her shop. It didn't take much in a small village to make yourself an enemy. 'Well,' she said languidly, stirring her matcha latte with one long, painted fingernail. 'Mark Tanner needs money.'

Carris shot Ruth a quizzical look. 'The man's as tight as they come. He must be loaded.'

Ruth narrowed her eyes. 'Loaded, but he's set up his own CashSplash page for this jaunt to Switzerland.'

Julia didn't feel it was right to call Mark's proposed trip a jaunt, but she said nothing since Ruth was continuing with barely a breath, heaping on a little extra unasked-for motive.

'Getting an exit visa on life is a pricey business.' The dress shop owner said, with a small smug smile.

'No.' Carris shook her head sadly. 'That doesn't work, Ruth. The fund is doing embarrassingly badly. He's only got a fiver in it, and it was me who put that in. I think people are finding it's a hard thing to donate for.' Carris rested her small, bird-like head at a thoughtful angle. 'It's not like he's asking for money for a treat or a registered charity.'

'I know what you mean,' Artie said, cautiously drawing out his chalked lines across Sal's daily coffee sign. 'I mean, I was happy to fund Mark's no-shoes day. That was fun. He raised two hundred quid for the Heart Foundation.'

'Isn't that wonderful?' Ruth said, and Julia wondered if she meant it.

'But Dignitas...' Artie shook his head. 'It can't be Mark that dobbed us in about the hay bales. I just don't believe it.' He stood back to admire his work, the neatly coiled cursive seeming to give him a feeling of sudden doubt.

Sal glanced over his shoulder. 'Oh.'

Artie turned. 'Oh?'

'Wrong two. You've got tea for too.'

Artie laughed, bringing out his duster and wiping off the errant "o". 'That's me all over. I can get the font perfect, but those letters, they're always jumping about, playing games.'

Suddenly, it dawned on Julia. 'Artie, did you write the new "No Callers" sign on the east gate at Hortishall?'

Artie laughed self-consciously. 'It was almost *Know* Callers.' The man beamed. 'That was me. Her Ladyship stood behind me the whole time, checking I got the letters in the right place. Sure, she got it wrong, though. She'd have to pay more for "know." A full two letters more than what she got. I charge by the digit. That woman might be rich, but she is as tight as it's possible to be without expiring herself out of life. The woman barely eats.'

Julia was barely listening any more, finding herself in the centre of a eureka moment as Artie droned on enthusiastically.

'So, she only wanted to pay for seven letters,' Artie

laughed knowingly, as though this was a problem he encountered all the time,' not the full nine. But I'm a perfectionist. I went up there late one night to just finish it off.'

'You were up at the Hall with Her Ladyship?' Carris asked, suddenly seeing where this was going.

Artie nodded. 'For hours. Her Ladyship was watching me the whole time.' He shivered. 'Bit too close for comfort if I'm being perfectly frank, so I was chatting with her about everything and anything; I mean, it's not like we have a lot of shared interests.' Artie lived in a caravan at the edge of the common, so it was easy to see his point. 'We'd just had the fete, and...' Suddenly, Artie's words started to dry on the tip of his tongue. Dry like a wave, pulling away from the seashore. 'We'd just had the fete, and I told her about...' he stuttered. His eyes widened. 'I told her about the hay bales.'

9

SELF-SERVICE

Two weeks later, the village was still digesting Lady Hortishall's news. Every single person in the town felt as though they were experiencing a severe case of acid reflux—some more than others. For those residing in the tithe cottages along the green, heartburn was a permanent fixture; they could think of nothing but the implementation of Her Ladyship's proposed barrier.

Poor Artie had been mortified at being the unsuspecting rat amongst the hay bales. Although, nobody blamed the man. It clearly wasn't his fault. For many, Her Ladyship's cruel manipulation of the innocent, typographically challenged, Artie fitted right in with their perception of Lady Hortishall as a woman who never gave a fig about fonts but was all too keen to stick the carving knife into a place over which she felt she had some kind of birthright. If the latest bombshell were to be believed, every single one of the Hortishall tithe cottages would be reverting back to the Hall. There would be no slides or fancy exiting apparatus needed because the entire string of low-rent housing would soon be traded out on the popular short-term letting agency AirMe&Thee, inhabited not by an ageing population of locals but a continual carousel of people pestering Maeve Masters at the Post Office for ripe avocados and designer granola.

In the wake of Her Ladyship's information explosion, it would appear everyone had forgotten about the promise of one-quarter of the Hortishall library's rare antiquities except from Julia. The village, sadly, had a lot more on its communal plate now than one small, prefabricated establishment for the borrowing of books. It was doubtful whether anything would ever be quite the same again. But as Brueghel depicted so well, and Auden picked up, turned around and poetically vomited onto his wonderful weft page—old masters were never wrong about suffering. Life went on. The sun still rose in the morning and set when the day was done.

So, on her way to work, Julia took herself a quick five minutes to make a stop at the Hall. The Mercedes was still on the drive. The stone eagles were still on their perch. Only now, the towering mansion looked very different. Beyond the gate, there was a great deal of activity. A team of contractors in neat white overalls, armed to the limb with high-tech machinery, were as busy as bunnies scarifying the lawn, replanting beds and cleaning Poseidon's throat as he lounged half-naked in the fountain at the Hall's main entrance. There was even a man up in the cedar, not stuck but simply removing some of the smaller branches that had withered and died over the winter months.

The contractors had left the gates open. The Hall was just a short hop, skip and peddle away. Julia could possibly reach it without being stopped. Despite the "Know Callers" sign hanging on one stone pillar (the sign which Artie - feeling duped - had edited back to his original design involving a "K"), Julia could have easily freewheeled down the drive towards the large oak doorway, lifted the heavy brass jaw of the green man knocker and confronted Her Ladyship.

The poor library manager had spent days disposing of the unwanted books that Her Ladyship had dumped on the local library's doorstep, returning them to the charity shop from which they had been bought. The assistant at the Heart Foundation seemed a little shocked to have the mildewed volumes all bounce back. Luckily, Carris' Bongo had meant that only one trip was needed. Julia and Carris had even helped the poor volunteer at the shop to re-shelf the books in alphabetical, vertically aligned shelving, using a system Julia herself had devised called the Rise and Shelf Tall Order System. In the end, the shop manager had been delighted, saying how the titles were looking neater than ever. With a sense of unavoidable pride, Julia had told the woman this was hardly surprising; they were qualified librarians and had taken multiple courses in shelving. They were, in fact, only a step short of a degree in alphabetising. Give them any letter in the alphabet, and she and Carris could move backwards, forwards, or in any direction of multiple leaps if instructed. It was, in fact, impossible to stump a librarian on their A, B, C.

The books that Julia and Carris' had carefully returned to the Heart Foundation were, of course, not the issue for which Julia needed an audience at the Hall. It was the promised antiquarian books that the library manager still hankered after, and that was what she wanted to talk to Her Ladyship about. Because Julia had noticed, when rescuing the cat, that the library at Hortishall Hall was completely bare. Only dust remained on the shelves. This was the terrible news that had sent Julia flying down Potter's Descent in search of Reece. Books like those in the Hortishall collection didn't just vanish.

For days now, Julia had diligently scanned the salerooms but to no avail; there were no listings of anything unusual. Certainly, nothing about the Eliot with the doodle of a butterfly, which surely would have generated nationwide interest. So, Julia had effortlessly put the facts together and figured that Her Ladyship must be storing the books somewhere. If the texts hadn't actually been sold, all was not lost. Therefore, all Julia had to do, in her capacity as library manager, was talk to Her Ladyship and make her see sense. With that accomplished, Julia had no doubt that she would take the final delivery of the books, which the small village library so rightfully deserved and so desperately needed. But tying Lady Hortishall down was proving problematic. Quite understandably, the woman was keeping a low profile.

Julia could imagine that if she did fast-foot it down the drive, past the gargling Poseidon, avoiding the falling branches from the cedar and up towards the oversized golden knocker, Lady Hortishall would not prove pleased to see her. Even without the army of garden contractors that had needed to be hired to when Curtis was 'let go', the woman had enough on her slim, bejewelled hands. Reece might be reluctant to challenge Lady Hortishall's perception of the ownership of the common, but Gemma was like a dog with a bone. She had been hard at work, examining case law from across the country. She contacted the HM Land Registry, The Historical Preservation of Landmarks and Litigation and the council's planning authority.

Gemma was leaving no stone unturned, not even (if she had her way) the stones where the eagles perched. However, it had been decided in the village not to make the matter public at the present. Everything was currently bubbling under the surface, hence the indigestion. Research had to be carried out before the dynamic young lawyer would feel confident in bringing such a large and serious case against the Hall's demands upon the common. The entire village had, therefore, agreed to keep quiet. Even Gareth at the Gazette had omitted to print the news. This may have been out of a genuine sense of community spirit, as the information would undoubtedly have been the scoop of a lifetime that Gareth was letting slip from his grasp, or it might have been because Gareth himself happened to be residing in one of the tithe cottages after the death of his late second uncle on his father's side. As Julia had always said, motivation didn't really matter. It was the outcome that was important. The outcome may still have been hanging in the balance, but its presence was overshadowing one and all in an air of hushed anticipation as the entire village prepared, waiting for the exact right moment when they would spring.

SADLY, however, Julia knew that this kind of case could take many years. Silas might well be dead by the time it was settled, and Julia herself would be long retired. So, although she didn't dare to admit it, the library manager knew she had to focus on her own battle. Her priority had to be ensuring the safety of the library by securing the whereabouts of the books, confronting Her Ladyship, and training Carris to cope with the day-to-day management of an establishment, which had a strangely uncompliant alarm system and a decidedly half-hearted band of library card holders.

This First Battle (a title Julia had awarded to the retrieval of the books) would be between Julia and Her Ladyship. It was a two-way thing and would not take an entire village or incur any spilling of the beans on Gemma's plan of action. Julia had been quietly making inroads since His Lordship's death, petitioning Lady Hortishall via the postal system. Unfortunately, she had not received one reply to any of the five letters she had sent. What Julia liked to think of as The Lost Letters was no longer of concern since the situation had changed—it had become more urgent. The books were no longer on the premises. This was a mystery and a problem. Julia decided to write a sixth letter, making it clear to the receiver that she had no intention of rolling over with a yawn and letting the books slip from her fingers. She would have to choose her words carefully. Words, Julia knew, were powerful things. Therefore, this morning, she would not hop, skip and peddle up to the Hall. She would not bang on its door. She would attack from a different angle with the pen, which was so much mightier than the fist on a knocker would ever be. Taking the handlebars of her trusty bike firmly between her wide, splayed fingers, Julia mounted the vehicle's seat and pushed off down Potter's Descent toward the direction of the village.

~

'Beautiful morning, Julia.' Clive called out from his cottage on the green as she cycled past.

It was true; the morning was glorious yet again. Lady Hortishall could do many things, but she could not switch off the weather or dampen the resilience of this small rural village.

As she glided through the town, Julia noticed Gemma on the street beside Mrs Talbot.

'But I'm feeling poorly,' the older woman was saying, leaning against her rusted Fiat Punto, which had been parked up outside Sal's in the disabled spot.

Gemma's brows knitted ferociously. 'You haven't got a disabled badge, and if you haven't got a badge, you're not poorly enough to be parking here.'

'Well,' Mrs Talbot raised her eyes in the attitude of a true martyr, one which the Reverend Tibbs and the almighty themselves would have been impressed by. 'Some of us just soldier on.'

Gemma shook her head. 'You need an official badge. You can't park here.'

Sadly, the power of the proposed legal action seemed to be going to poor Gemma's head. It was very difficult, Julia knew, to step back from the reins of power when it was being thrust on you left, right and centre.

'Morning ladies,' Julia called as she sped past, just catching Mrs Talbot's feeble reply to the off-the-clock lawyer.

'But I do have such a terrible pain in my... earlobe.'

Julia tried to suppress an ironic smile; Mrs Talbot, the old faker, would never win.

~

'MOVE IT, GEOFF.' Julia rang her bell as she approached the library. Its bright, happy sound echoed down the narrow, tarmacked road. 'You're early today?'

Geoff hunched his large shoulders and took a step to the side so that Julia could slide her bike into the lock.

'Mum kicked me out. Said I was getting under her feet. I thought I could help do a bit of shelving of something.'

Unlikely, Julia thought, but when the words came out of her mouth, they sounded much more akin to 'lovely.'

'Any news on the common?' Geoff asked eagerly.

'Shh, Geoff.' Julia glanced around anxiously. 'I don't know the ins and outs, but Gemma and the team are keeping it quiet and asking us all to do the same.'

The would-be journalist in Geoff looked disappointed.

'That means no YouTubing about the predicament.' Julia said, knowing that with Geoff, it was always best to spell it out. Independent filmmakers were notoriously tricky on the keeping it shtum. They just can't help themselves from wanting to blab, digitally or otherwise. She slid her keys into the old blue door, with its wide glass window, pushing through it with her shoulder. She grabbed the broom as she passed and gave the alarm a swift poke.

'You are so nifty with that.' Geoff said, his voice full of admiration.

Julia wondered to herself, as she returned the broom to the wall, if a young man like Geoff should really be turning his admiration elsewhere, but she said nothing. It was not her business to judge. Besides, admiration of any kind when you were over sixty was short on the ground. 'I'm still not open yet, Geoff. You're early.' She said with a small, involuntary huff. In truth, Julia wished Geoff wasn't there; she'd come in way before nine so she could get her letter written —her very important letter to Her Ladyship, and there was no way she could get started on that with Geoff hanging lurch-like over her shoulder.

'I don't mind waiting.' Geoff said, without bothering to go back outside.

She would just have to make the best of it. Julia glanced

across the shelves in front of her, puffing out her chest a little, readying herself for an action she relished. 'I thought I'd find a couple of books that were needed.' She said, running her eyes along the shelving that she knew so well before walking towards the Self-Help section and raising one hand in the direction of a neat line of vertically compliant titles.

Behind her, Geoff watched, puzzled.

'On my way in...' she said, by way of explanation, 'I noticed Gemma was looking a little stressed. Taking a tad too much law to the street.' Julia pulled *How to Avoid Alienating Friends and Family* by Doctor Smart-Alec from the place where it always stood in the "A" section. She'd recommended Dr Alec before. For a medical practitioner, he had a comedic way of looking at the world. A way which could often aid in the dissolution of the day-to-day trials and tribulations of village life. Though perhaps a lightweight for the Hortishall confrontation, Smart-Alec had worked wonders on the leylandii debacle, and Julia felt that Gemma would need a little something to calm her down over the following weeks. When you get to threatening old ladies in the street, even if they deserve it, you need to take time out. Besides, it was necessary for Gemma to be concentrating her efforts elsewhere.

'Oh, that looks good.' Geoff said, eagerly eyeing Dr Smart-Alec's cover, depicting a serious man with overlarge glasses, a wild expression in his eyes, and an unusual way of wearing a stethoscope whilst walking a tightrope, holding a set of scales and a seal. Julia had always wondered at the relevance of the seal. There was certainly a lot going on. But all of that was beside the point. Julia turned towards Geoff, curious. She was unable to resist slipping into a different type of balancing act - one that all library managers do instinctively - weighing up each potential reader with potential books. It was a habit she found it impossible to divest herself of and one which was becoming increasingly difficult since the advent of self-publishing.

Smart-Alec in hand, Julia wondered about the balance in front of her—Geoff certainly had form on the alienation front. Stick a camera in a person's face or record their words in the pub, and it tends to get people's backs up. Yes, the book-to-person fit worked. She smiled sweetly. 'After Gemma reads it, Geoff, it's yours.' She slid the book onto the desk for when Gemma would come in later. 'And there was one more thing...' Julia hooked her bottom lip under her teeth and cast her mind back to Mrs Talbot. There must be something in the library that could aid the old lady out as well, put her on the right track.

Julia wandered back to the Self-Help section, a section which had been growing rapidly over the past few years. This was causing no end of concern for the library HQ. Soon, illnesses would be push fiction off the shelves and making an inroad into biography. Perhaps that would be the way of it; classifications would simply blur. Medical Romances had certainly made a good transition—bridging the gap between a kiss and the threat of an irritating rash or two. Illness was a big twenty-first-century preoccupation. Maladies cropped up everywhere, and everyone wanted to self-diagnose. Seven years of medical training be damned. All people needed now was a pained, vaguely symmetrical face, good hair, straight teeth, access to a free streaming channel and an appropriate book referral—fiction or otherwise. Every day, there was some startling success story of self-diagnosis. No one was interested in sending people to the moon anymore; all they wanted was a cure for an irritating but persistent personal condition. This, however, was not Mrs Talbot's problem. Mrs T's situation was entirely different. The woman had been complaining about her earlobes, which was unusual since the earlobe had no nerve endings. Suddenly, Julia noticed exactly what she needed—a large volume sitting on a high shelf. She turned back to Geoff, who had, after all, said he was there to help. 'Would you do the honours?'

'Sure.' The lad lumbered forward with his arms dangling and leather jacket creaking.

Julia stood back to let him pass, bathed in a sudden sea of cheap aftershave along with the canned smell of a liberally applied deodorant before Geoff reached up, as agile as a ballerina. It was clear that the man was in desperate need of a dedicated activity, something to get him focused and give him poise. A purpose was all Geoff needed to switch him from a lumbering lout to a graceful gazelle. A dedicated occupation could never be underestimated in the definition of self, Julia thought to herself, as Geoff lifted the tome down.

'*How to Keep Your Doctor on His Toes? 500 Maladies You Never Knew Existed*,' the lad read, nodding thoughtfully as if this book really was the bee's knees.

Julia smiled, satisfied. 'That should do it.'

Suddenly, Geoff's jaw dropped open on its hinges, his eyes taking on the appearance of oddly protruding ping-pong balls. 'That is some serious bum-arse madness,' he said, his features leaching to a confused, off-the-scale shade of white as he glanced over Julia's shoulder.

'Geoff!' Julia had never heard the expression 'bum-arse madness' before and wasn't entirely sure what it meant if it made sense, or even if it was orthographically accurate.

'Julia. Look!' Geoff continued staring behind her,

pointing one long, leather-clad spectre-of-death-type arm back into the room.

Expecting to see nothing in particular (Geoff did like to exaggerate), Julia turned and promptly found her own jaw dropping to the floor. For there, in front of her, standing just shy of the kiddie's corner, was a large person-sized black box. Julia's first thought was that it must be more of Her Ladyship's tricks. Thirty boxes in all had arrived. They might still be arriving if Julia hadn't stuck a sign on the library door herself, clearly stating, "Pulp-fiction paperbacks not welcome." But somehow, this box was different. It was far more proper for a start. It wasn't sagging cardboard picked up from the no-longer-needed pile at the Spa shop. The thing standing directly before Geoff and Julia was metal, more obelisk than a box.

'What on earth is that?' Julia said loudly, all whispers to the wind. She took a step forward over the brightly covered playtime rug (suitable for hiding all manner of stains) towards the black graphite rectangle.

'A box.' Geoff replied promptly.

Julia turned briefly to shoot him a wry look. 'For a man of few words, Geoff, sometimes you don't half hit the nail on the head.'

Geoff nodded, satisfied, a flick of a smile hovering over his full lips before his brow crosshatched, and he glanced nervously towards the door. 'But how did they get this...' he said, rapping on the top of the obelisk, '...through the letterbox?'

Julia gave the young man another stare, far less appreciative. 'Think you might just have overextended yourself there, Geoff.' She reached into her handbag for her phone. Luckily, she had Carris on speed dial. 'Carris?' Julia said, knowing, of course, that it was Carris at the other end of the line. The young woman was infamously single with the social life of a pair of slippers. 'You need to get yourself down here on the double.'

It was a Thursday—Carris' late morning in, but that didn't matter now. Julia needed all minds at the ready. Even Carris' quarter quota of standard-issue grey material might help. Someone was playing silly buggers.

'Do you think it's a Kubrick fan?' Geoff asked hopefully. 'It's a bit *2001: A Space Odyssey*.'

'Really quick, Carris,' Julia said, knowing that it was only a matter of time before Geoff would be asking if the library budget could extend to monkeys and large sticks. 'Just put your foot down hard on the Bongo's go-faster peddle and get yourself in here pronto.' She didn't wait for a reply. Julia clicked off her phone, hoping that the wind would be behind Carris, giving her that little extra speed that was so needed on trips out in the Bongo. Julia took another look at the black box, drinking it all in. Speed was crucial now because this truly was the beginning of the end.

'Do you know where I can find *The Lord of the Rings*?' Geoff mumbled, bored already.

'Middle Earth,' the library manager said without even a hint of irony.

~

'So,' Carris peered at the box. 'Educated guess?'

'That would be good, Carris.' Julia nodded. 'But as there's no one else around, I'll settle for your opinion.'

Undeterred, Carris took herself on a full circle of the large, black, rectangular box. 'It's big,' she offered sagely.

Julia sighed. 'Is that the best you can do, Carris—big?'

Carris' eyes narrowed resolutely. 'It's got to be something to do with Lady Hortishall.'

Since the diddling on the books and the attempted invasion of the common, Lady Hortishall was being blamed for everything. Her reputation preceded her in just about every area of life, taking on gargantuan proportions. Give her enough time, and the woman would be souring the milk from the cows and blighting the crops in the field. That was often how these things started. A little resentment can go a long way.

'No,' Julia said shortly. 'This has nothing to do with Her Ladyship. More's the pity. This...' Julia waved one arm towards the black tower '...is Pandora's box.'

Carris' face soured in frustration. 'Well, she'll just have to come and collect it. We can't have people dumping their things...'

'I think...' Geoff said awkwardly, clearing his throat and shifting from foot to foot. 'I think Julia's referring to Pandora in Greek mythology.'

'Thank you, Geoff.' Julia gave the young lad a quick, surreptitious thumbs up. 'Pandora, with her box full of beasties.'

'Oh,' Carris took a step back, imagining no doubt a tower of Indiana-Jones-style creepy crawlies eager to burst out of their steel chest. 'I'll get pest control in.'

Julia rolled her eyes before tapping hard on the metal lid. 'It's a self-service machine, Carris. Nothing to do with insect eradication. This is you in the not-too-distant future.'

Carris' eyes practically ping-ponged out of her head as though the things were on springs. 'Well, what's happened to my hips?'

'I think...' Geoff cleared his throat once again. 'Julia is talking metaphorically.'

'Thank you, Geoff, for that epiphany of enlightenment there.' Julia said, attempting to keep the sarcasm out of her voice with a narrow miss. Narrow enough, that was, for Geoff to remain blissfully ignorant.

The young lad beamed. 'You know, filmmaking and books, they're not so different. I could work...'

'No.' Julia and Carris said at the exact same moment, in the exact same affirmative tone. Julia knew that the occasional flash of insight and the ability to converse with a handful of long words, slipping them into the conversation with serendipitous alacrity, did not make a good worker. 'Only on the Valuable Volunteer scheme. Geoff. As I've told you before, we are fully staffed, and if Mr Perkins at head office has his way...' Julia tapped the top of the box, 'soon young Carris and I will also be obsolete.'

This was a total conversation killer. For what seemed like a good five minutes, Julia, Carris and Geoff stood stock-still looking at the future—the black box with its electronic arm for logging in and bucket-like belly for dropping off. Could it all really be that easy? They stood until Carris coughed uneasily into the library silence, thankfully bringing them back from this seemingly apocalyptic future. 'So, what now?'

Julia cast her eyes down, rubbing at her chin thoughtfully. 'I'm thinking, Carris.' She did this often and was normally very good with the process. But if truth be told, Julia was all out of good ideas.

'We could tow it out onto the common,' Geoff said, his voice all enthusiasm, relishing in the idea of letting the thing free.

'That's fly-tipping, Geoff.' Julia said curtly. 'And how that common is being watched now, you'd be arrested before you'd slid the boxes of plastic black coasters out of the back of Carris' Bongo. No. We must hide it.' Julia said, pleased with her sudden inspiration. 'Hide it in plain sight, then deny all knowledge.'

'Oh, I do like that.' Carris clapped her hands together in excitement—an excitement which set the oddly jangling necklace she was wearing swinging precariously. 'I'll get the little ones to knock up some artwork when they come in after the school drop-off. That should do the trick. They're very prolific.'

This was true, although Julia thought calling the efforts of the under-fives "artwork" was a stretch.

'Onward and upward.' Carris said lightly. 'And, in all the excitement, Julia...' Carris preened. 'You forgot to comment on my new outfit.'

Julia had not, in fact, forgotten to pass comment on Carris' present attire; not talking about the outfit was more a case of tactful avoidance. But now that she was being asked to report, flattery failed her. 'Sorry, Carris, but there's only so much fun my retinas can take, and they reached their limit at the cardigan.'

'Oh, too much?' Carris said, looking critically down at her small, thin body and the screaming yellow cardi stripped with neon green that she happened to be sporting.

'I suppose the question is why,' Julia said, ignoring the fashion statement and sweeping the dropped books from the carpet in front of the library door before readying herself to stick out the welcome sign.

Carris nodded eagerly. 'Oh, there's a reason, Julia. It's all part of a master plan.'

Geoff's ears pricked up, and an excited glint fired up in his eyes.

'Apparently,' Carris continued, 'Mr Perkins is doing his rounds.'

'The regional manager.' Geoff said in a hushed tone of awe, which sounded a bit like a bad voiceover.

Julia was just about to tell Geoff to knock it off and keep his theatricals until a project got green-lit when she suddenly realised that Carris might have somehow said something astute. Julia had not been talking about the outfit. Naturally, her concerns were on the box, only now it appeared that Carris' outfit and the box might, in fact, be connected. 'So, he's doing his rounds, and that's why we got the box?'

'No,' Carris raised her eyes to the heavens. 'Perkins is doing his rounds, so that's why I wore the cardi,' Carris enthused. 'And the shoes, and the matching handbag and...'

Julia held up one hand. 'Enough.'

'He's single, you know.'

Julia did not, in fact, know this. Truth be known, the man was a bit of a mystery. No one had seen him outside of head office. There were no photographs on the website. There had been no press release in the papers. The man was fond of secrecy, of catching unwitting library managers unawares. No one knew when it would be their turn next.

'I was thinking maybe I'd get him to fall in love with me,' Carris said wistfully. 'Then stick him in the Bongo and go off on a tour of Europe.'

Julia's eyes narrowed. It felt a little as though Carris was missing the point here. However, Julia sometimes had to admire her young library assistant for her Beaux-Arts attitude to life—life goes on. 'Is he short then?'

'Oh, Julia.' Carris laughed. 'You are such a card. As long as he bends at the knees and ideally at the neck, we'll manage.'

'What about the common?' Julia knew she had to get

Carris back on track. The admiration was done. This was not a time to be getting flaky.

'Gemma said the common could take years to sort,' Carris said dismissively.

Julia felt her features hardening and a cloud of bitter determination descending. 'What about solidarity on the library front?' she said, trying her hardest to keep her voice level. 'I'm going to be retiring soon. Ideally sooner than planned. You can't go "Bongoing" off all around Europe.'

'Oh, don't worry about the retirement do. I'm all up for that.' Carris flashed a carefree wrist in Julia's direction.

Julia hadn't even thought about her retirement do.

'I think we'll do it in the Dog and Duck. Sal's is too small, the village hall a trifle cold, and Regi said he wouldn't charge us a hire cost for the function room above the bar.'

Julia was feeling shocked, not realising that all this planning had been going on without her.

'Angie said she'd bring her cider press down. I said no to Beatrice Bells' organ. Regi was having none of it, and Salvatori secretly,' Carris lowered her voice, 'says he'll sing, but only if Beatrice's organs don't make an appearance. Any of them. Even the little ones with the tubular bells.'

Julia felt her mind swimming. She leaned over and clutched the desk.

'I said you'd be making a speech.' Carris pinched her shoulders together in a shrug. 'Reverend Tibbs offered to do it, but you know what he's like for putting his foot in everything. So, I told him, Julia...' Carris said, her eyes dancing up to the ceiling as though trying to retrieve her moment with the reverent. 'I told him that actually, you are library manager, have been for over thirty years, and as such, your way with words is exemplary.'

Silence fell once again in the library.

'Have you finished?' Julia said.

'Oh no,' Carris laughed. 'There's a lot of planning, Julia. This is going to be the event of the decade. Gareth's already drawn up his headline.'

Julia slumped down in the seat. It squeaked behind her, its back rocking awkwardly. 'But, Carris...' she said, unable to keep the shock out of her words. 'I'm not going for a while yet, and there are other matters...' Julia slowed her voice and sharpened her diction so that none of the import of her words would be lost. 'Other matters of key importance to the village, to the library.'

'Well, yes, exactly.' Carris said, her features taking on a serious hue. 'That's why I wanted to fit my trip to Europe in before you went. Rest assured, Julia.' Carris rested her hand on the older librarian's shoulder. 'I'll be back to hold the reins. Not a problem, Julia. You can count on me.'

Julia wasn't sure that she could. She wasn't sure that all the planning wasn't just a step too far or that, in truth, Carris could even count on herself. However, she couldn't help but be secretly impressed by the organisational structure which Carris had been quietly putting in place. Julia was a pragmatist and was all too aware that sometimes it was necessary to let a person, a person like Carris, stand on their own two feet and overreach a little on the self-belief front. The retirement party seemed to be an occasion in which Carris was overreaching and yet coming out smelling of daisies. However, there were other important issues at play here. It was highly unlikely that Carris would persuade Mr Perkins, who, despite being unmarried, was a man Carris had never met. Therefore, it seemed a stretch-too-far of any kind of reality that Mr Perkins would be tempted of a six-month sabbatical around Europe in the Bongo. It was far more likely that the man would be spending the summer wheeling out his warehouse of automata—the self-service armies which would replace each and every library manager in the county. 'We can't let ourselves be replaced by automation, Carris. People will miss the human touch.'

'Everybody saw those lights in the sky.' Geoff piped up inappropriately.

'Geoff, I told you before, when you got that bee in your bonnet about the lights over Reece's house. That was temporary security. You got yourself in hot water then, and you'll get yourself in it again if you keep going all X-Files.' Julia sighed. 'If aliens did go landing here, they've lost their way. Take my word for it: nobody is being body-snatched or invaded by cosmic entities in the middle of rural nowhere. What is happening is that we are being replaced. We will be the casualties—the atrophy of atomisation.'

A puzzled look flitted across Geoff's face.

Carris looked idly at the box. 'I guess you're right then, Julia. It would be a shame if they replaced people with machines. No one's going to get much conversation out of that.'

Julia couldn't help but feel a small twinge somewhere at the back of her mind—a twinge which was asking if maybe that wasn't such a bad thing after all. Certainly, discussions in the library were often circuitous, seemingly pointless, containing a great deal of moaning, a splattering of warmth and bonhomie, and one hell of a lot of dobbing in. A self-service machine couldn't do that. Julia sighed, the weight of the century seeming suddenly heavy upon her shoulders. She glanced around her at the books lining the walls and at her desk piled high with assessment forms waiting to be filed. The library needed to be sorted. They would be opening the doors soon. The counter would be on above the blue entrance, with its wide glass window registering the footfall; business would begin. They could not fight the future—the machine. However, the library was an important space. There were other fights that needed to be set in motion—Julia had an important letter to write to Lady Hortishall. Tackling the disappearance of the books was the sort of triumph that a human could only win, and Julia had no intention of letting it slip from her hands.

~

'Do you think it should be sincerely, yours truly, or best wishes?' Julia asked. The day was almost done. Mr Perkins had not arrived. The self-service machine had been covered in the "artwork" of at least fifteen preschoolers. The camouflage would not last forever, but it might well buy them a bit of time.

Carris paused momentarily in her task of shelving a cartload of returned volumes, a Sisyphean occupation in a small rural library. 'My goodness, Julia. All these letters you keep writing. Who are you posting them to?'

Julia didn't want to answer this question, so she hastily put her blue writing paper under a handy copy of *Dangerous Liaisons*.

'I'm just practising my calligraphy.' Julia said with a brightness she simply did not feel.

'Aren't you clever,' Carris said admiringly, and Julia wondered if Carris had any idea what calligraphy was. 'I guess,' Carris sucked in a thin line of air, raising her large eyes to the ceiling in thought. 'It depends on the letter. Is it another condolence one? Or is it a thank you? Or is it...' Carris twirled her eyes around the library as though hunting for inspiration. 'A kind of get-off-my-land-type missive?'

Again, Julia was struck by Carris' perspicuity. Although this was not a 'land' issue, there was a definite parallel. 'General, ballpark,' Julia said thoughtfully, 'I'd say, the "get off my land" vein.'

Carris nodded. 'Very popular at the moment. In that case...' Her eyes narrowed in a serious attitude. 'Sincerely,' she said with unusual decisiveness. 'Sincerely, has that killer edge to it. It's the sibilance. It makes it quite snake-like. Viperish. Mess with me, and there will sincerely be serious consequences.'

And for once, Julia had to agree that Carris was right —*sincerely* did have the punch that was needed.

10

THE DELIVERY

The day was shifting into the evening by the time Julia found herself standing beneath the gaze of the large stone eagles. She'd hung about at the library for hours, hoping that the contractors would be gone by the time she got to the Hall, but the hired hands were clearly a determined lot on the weeding front. Despite the dwindling light, the place looked immaculate. One of the white-overalled men was even following the flatbed truck with a rake as the vehicle pulled down the drive, smoothing over the gravel so there would be not a trace of tyres messing with the crushed stones. It was impossible not to be impressed.

The men all gave Julia a wave as they trundled out of the drive and onto the road. She waved politely back, telling them not to worry about locking the gate behind them; she'd shut it herself. This, for some odd reason, seemed to make them all inordinately happy. As though the gate-shutting had always been a step too far on the contractual front, and they simply couldn't wait to get down the pub, peel off their leaf-splattered jackets and sink a pint or two. As the vehicles trundled past, Julia joined in the bonhomie amiably enough, even if she didn't fully understand it. Julia was all too aware that with an emotion like bonhomie, it was always best to jump in with both feet and a smile. There was even a book advocating just this at the library: *Bonhomie or Bust: A Humorous Quest for Social Acceptance* by Felix Droll. Felix was a bit long-winded if truth be known, taking himself eighty thousand words to explain a concept which could be summed up in a sentence. This hadn't stopped Julia from attempting to push the volume into Geoff's hands on numerous occasions. Unfortunately, it didn't have any pictures, and it had always proved a stretch trying to get Geoff to indulge in anything but the illustrated. However, this evening, Julia had other things on her mind as she watched the caravan of vehicles disappearing over the horizon of Potter's Descent. She watched till they'd pulled every last puff of diesel smoke along with them. She watched until the sound of their heavy tyres on the tarmac and the jangle of their assorted kit - leaf blowers, rakes, trimmers, chainsaws, shovels, spades and an unprecedented array of working wheelbarrows - clashing and rattling inside of the vans stilled. In fact, Julia watched until all sounds of the Horticultural Hegemony had faded like a charm into a rustle of leaves stirred by the welcome kiss of the evening's light breeze, and somewhere in the woods beside the Hall, a nightingale struck up its tune. She watched till there was no more memory of the men. She waited until she knew she was alone because, in all honesty, Julia wasn't exactly sure how Her Ladyship was going to take a house call from the library manager.

It was a common misconception that the upper classes were not keen on outbursts. It was generally assumed that those with a paid education had been taught milder manners and were, therefore, less prone to animated rants and volatile vitriol. This delusion was based on a fallacy perpetuated by the marketing department of the independent school system—a system whose interest was served by keeping quiet about the constant brawling of the boarding hall dorms. It was a fallacy further perpetuated by the fact that part and parcel of being a member of the landed gentry was that you would live in a large house with plenty of space for full-on flare-ups of fury. It was also a well-known fact that, along with Latin, you would receive an in-depth education on rugby. Despite the common misconception, this was not so that you could support the England team or wear a rugger shirt without feeling like a fraud. No. This was so that you could swiftly dispatch unwanted traders with a trained tackle. Julia knew this all too well. Lady Hortishall could easily get nasty and grab her in a scrum. It was unlikely, but one should never underestimate a grieving widow with a private education. Julia also knew, however, that in making her request for the books, she was within her rights. She was being reasonable. Her voice needed to be heard. However, erring on the side of caution, since nobody liked a public fray, she had waited till well after the last puff of contractors disappeared over the horizon line of Potter's Descent before scooting slowly towards the door.

She stood on the doorstep for a good fifteen minutes, waiting for the large oak door to be pulled back. She had lifted the golden lower lip of the green man knocker a total of ten times. Each time, she gained a little confidence in the number of raps she doled out, the pressure of the rap, and the noise level said rap emitted. After fifteen minutes, Julia had reached a pattern of seventeen very loud knocks and couldn't get the popular, emancipatory tune "Eye of the Tiger" out of her head. A tune which was, perhaps, curiously fitting. And yet, still, the door didn't open. Yes, Julia had the letter, but she had wanted to talk. She had wanted to gauge Lady Hortishall's reaction. Questions needed answering, a Last Will and Testament that needed honouring and the mystery as to where the books were. It was surely not possible to make an entire library vanish into thin air. However, it would appear that Her Ladyship was not playing ball—not even the elliptical, pigskin type. The battle would have to be resumed at a later date. Feeling an overwhelming sense of disappointment, but always the pragmatist, Julia pushed the gapping slot of the golden letterbox flap open and slipped the blue envelope through.

Tomorrow was another day, she thought to herself as she cycled away from the house. Perhaps Her Ladyship took strong sedatives and was already sleeping. Perhaps the woman was out. Perhaps Lady Hortishall was hard of hearing or sporting noise-cancelling headphones in an attempt to block out the gardeners or had incurred a head injury on the playing fields of her childhood. There were a million reasons why someone wouldn't open a door. Most of them were innocent. Tomorrow, Julia would stop in on her way to the library. Her Ladyship would have received the letter and had time to think over its contents. Perhaps this was indeed the best way to approach the matter. They would both get to sleep on it and with the catchy earworm tune that Rocky Bilboa loved so well, Julia pushed off on her bike and freewheeled down the hill. Tomorrow, all would be well.

~

ONLY, the next day, the normally oh-so-quiet flat strip of tarmac echoed not with bird song but with sirens. The police drove in a line like a spray of caterpillars on amphetamines. Their blue lights flared and bounced off the green wall of leylandii as they nearly knocked poor Julia out of their path in their haste.

Confused, the library manager stopped and pushed her toes into the soft, springy September earth so that her bike was fully supported, and she watched curiously as the vehicles trailed past in their long, steady procession. Four of them. The wheels of her brain whirred. *Four.* One, they could be delivering news or investigating a natural tragedy. They had sent one car, Julia remembered, when Lord Hortishall had snored his last. Two, it could be something simpler, like an attempted burglary. Even though most of the expensive garden machinery had gone off on the flatbeds the night before, there were certainly things within the house worth taking. Three, maybe it was tax evasion. His Lordship did spend an inordinate amount of time over at Reece's. But four? As Julia knew all too well, police cars had their own semaphoric system, just as sure as magpies. This had all been laid out in black and white within the highly controversial pages of *Cracking the Cop Culture*. Written by Smokey Breaker, a CB Radio enthusiast, it was a volume which had been banned from the Suffolk library system after a number of the force had complained about being surveilled. But Julia had given it a quick once over before the publication got redacted. Therefore, she was all too aware that four cars had to mean something far more sinister than a heart stopping, or a few candlesticks being shifted from a marble mantlepiece. Four cars meant murder.

Instantly, Julia's heart appeared to jump up uninvited from her chest to her throat. For a moment, the woman could barely breathe. *Murder*—she thought to herself as her face paled to wax, and she scouted forward. She scouted far enough so that she was positioned, once again, under the glare of the stone eagles. Positioned just in the right place to see the police banging the heavy oak door down and tumbling through the wide entrance Hall in a pile of shouts and boots and truncheons, tumbling, no doubt, over the blue envelope she had pushed through the golden letter box only the night before.

11

FALL OUT

'Dead?' Sal slipped a large mug of strong tea, heavy on the sugar, across the rickety wooden table towards the poor, aghast Julia. Julia rarely drank tea. Her tastes on the hot beverage front were of a more continental inclination, but this morning, only tea or a shot of something far stronger would pull off the necessary—warm the librarian back into life. And, although there was little evidence of it at present (Julia was barely moving), sooner or later, the woman would need to leave the coffee shop and get back into the world and onto her bike. The day waited for no one. Therefore, a tot of whisky had to be a no-no. PC Mumblings might well be otherwise engaged up at the Hall, but everybody knew that the man was a jobsworth. Mumblings would soon be out combing the streets from the air-conditioned environment of his Panda. His slim, constabulary-issued dictation device was never far from those curiously large lips. The lips were as bloated as two fat pink slugs from the man's unnatural predilection for tannoy usage. It was a device Mumblings would resort to whenever and wherever possible; the man liked nothing more than hollering a few well-chosen rules and regulations at the general public-especially when he caught them unawares. It was an unfortunate habit that he had never shaken off from his childhood days—when young Mumblings had terrorised the general population from the graphite grey footboard of his scooter. "Officious" was practically the man's middle name and no doubt Mumblings would dearly love any opportunity to pull Julia over to the side and charge her with a DUI before lording himself up on the airways of the local law enforcement agencies, bragging about having two police incidents in the short space of an eight-hour shift. It would make the man's year—possibly even his decade (he had little going on). Never mind that Julia's vehicle only had two wheels and a maximum speed of ten miles per hour when operated by the cautious, over-sixties librarian—a woman who also happened to have extensive expertise in the highway code on account of the sixth-former's after school club held every Wednesday in the IT section of the library.

Sadly, the man would delight in catching her out. He was a red tape enthusiast. At the thought of something ribbon-like and possessing the possibility to cordon, Julia found herself gripped in an involuntary shiver. The concerned Sal mistook the shiver for a drop in body temperature on account of the recent shock the librarian had experienced and instantly broke out the fan heater kept under the café counter for the winter months. To hell with the exorbitant costs associated with running the thing, or its propensity to dry out the atmosphere, the Bath buns and even the (much prized) sourdough—needs must. However, unknown to Sal, Julia's shiver had nothing to do with the shock or the temperature. No, Julia's shiver was prompted by an entirely different provenance. It was simply the thought of tape.

This morning, the woman had no desire to reflect on any kind of tape in relation to the police—not with the sound of an ambulance still ringing in her ears and the imagined on-repeat GIF of a blue envelope lying abandoned on the welcome mat of the Hall. The said image had ear-wormed itself in uninvited, repeating frenetically as the chimes of an automated monkey, clashing its symbols through poor Julia's brain. This was, in fact, not only irritating but ludicrous. For the Hortishall's possessed no such mat, and the monkey was purely fictitious. Yet still, the conjured image of the library manager's blue envelope lying abandoned on the coarse coir hairs of the imaginary Hortishall hospitality rug haunted the unfortunate, shell-shocked Julia.

In fact, for a good five minutes, the woman could barely get any words out of her mouth. Not one. It was an unusual occurrence, and, therefore, this silence did not go unnoticed. The long-standing manager of the small rural library was well-known county-wise for being a linguistic virtuoso on the discourse front. She was a woman able to play the keys of conversation with a situational fine-tuning and finesse that would have left Mozart himself impeded on the old ivories and Cyrano reaching for a little Bergerac in the hope of getting his infamously superior vocal instrument piping on par. Even the razor-sharp-witted Elizabeth Bennet of *Pride and Prejudice*, the bonnet-wearing heroine of so many a young girl's heart, would have fallen short if pitched against Julia in a face-off rap-slam. However, not this morning—this morning, Julia's jaw was slack. Her habitually flushed powdered features appeared as pale as a marshmallow—the large gelatinous white ones that had busted their sides and cracked their faces. The shock had wiped out every inch of human expression from poor Julia's very being.

As was only natural in a small rural village with a fluctuating population of around two thousand, three hundred and sixty-three souls, there had been death in the community before. For anyone needing to get a wider historical perspective, it was necessary to go no further than the combined classes of years five, six and seven currently taking their studies at St Martin's in the Meadows—the rural Primary School. It had an Ofsted rating of "inadequate" due to its propensity to cram three year groups, complete with gerbils, into one classroom a piece, learning about The Great Fire of London, The Battle of Britain and the curiously compelling tale of Samuel Pepys and his buried parmesan (an event so treasured by the British education system that it warranted a repeat every year, which caused a run on the Co-op's meagre selection of hard dairy products). Along with all of the aforesaid educational directives, there was one other favoured subject. It was relished so fondly by the school and the entire UK population that each of the thirty or so pupils in the top tier of the local School would have been more than happy to spout forth on it to anyone with more than a passing interest. A period of history does not get to go under the heading "The Black Death" without involving a bizarrely alluring elevated expiration rate.

However, putting pandemics to one side, you would only have to take a stroll through the graveyard to see that the broad, flat blade of a shovel was needed most years. Recently, there had been a number of locals checking out early. The most notable this very year had been Mia Chung, a young widow who had failed to get through the winter.

Everyone had told Mia that it was a bad idea to try to unicycle across the large frozen pond at the bottom of her garden, not when she hadn't even mastered her gravitational centre point when cycling through the more predictable lanes. Unicycling was a notoriously difficult sport involving core strength and coordination, neither of which Mia Chung had. Despite the common conception, single-wheel pursuits were not for clowns. This was a misrepresentation deliberately perpetuated by the IFC (The International Federation of Clowning) designed to encourage the bored middle classes, known for their whimsical natures and ungoverned cash splurges, to buy themselves unicycles, only to sell the contraptions a few weeks later, via the classified ads, at knockdown prices. Clowns had always been known for their empty pockets and their love of a bargain.

Surprisingly, Mia had been persistently struggling with her one-wheeled vehicle for some months. Although unsteady, the young woman was clearly making progress. Gareth had even told the advertisers at the Gazette not to hold any ad space for the vehicle. It looked as if young Mia was going to make it. But, alas, the ice, coupled with her insistence on chainsaw juggling, had proved a step too far. As was often the case with incidents of this nature, the whole thing had to be hushed up quickly. Although no charges were ever pressed, it transpired that the young (still grieving) Mia had actually lifted the power machinery from Curtis' shed when he was out. It could have been on account of Mia's diminished responsibility after the passing of her partner, but most likely, the always frugal Ms Chung had been reluctant to incur more cost, especially since she had no idea if she would be able to pull the tricky, though visually spectacular, manoeuvre with the heavy hand-held machinery off.

It was only when Curtis went looking for his handheld equipment that poor Mia had been discovered. Being a man of few words, having sympathy with the woman's predicament, and not being fond of the law (a law presided over by PC Mumblings), Curtis had not reported the missing equipment. The theft had been forgotten. Sadly, the ramifications did not stop there; it had been difficult getting Mia out of the ice since the only chainsaw in the village was also frozen into a cold, crystal rectangle. Nobody had been comfortable about leaving the unfortunate woman to thaw out in the village hall, commonly known as the Harmony Hut, due to the regular choral meetings on a Tuesday and a Thursday. But the body had to go somewhere, and so the hut got taken over. Luckily, Dr Carter was categorically convinced that going by the young woman's body weight and local weather conditions, Mia should be nicely thawed out by Monday evening. Therefore, it was only the Scouts who would be inconvenienced—the troop always met on a Monday, and even though every one of the Scouts insisted they weren't squeamish, caretaker Clive Corpusty put his foot down.

Many people felt Clive had other motivations rather than protecting the impressionable minds of the young. It was common knowledge that Clive had never been fond of organised activities for boys. He felt there was an oxymoron at play here and that boys could not, in fact, be organised. Apart from linguistic paradox, there were other factors which the caretaker brought into his argument. Boys, he claimed, were prone to tramping mud and snow into 'his' hall, not to mention the pushing of folded sweet wrappers into the radiator vents. Megan Keeble had argued with Clive on many occasions about this very matter, claiming staunchly that these activities were not gender specific. Many females and non-binary youngsters had muddy soles, and if a radiator had grills, it was almost impossible for anyone under the age of twelve to resist shoving something small and folded into the mesh. However, Clive stated, in no uncertain terms, that he wasn't interested in anything Megan had to say.

In the end, the Reverend Tibbs, in true Christian spirit, had announced that the Scouts would be welcome to use the church on the Monday in question, provided they didn't mess with the crucifixes. Death, the clergyman said, was a constant reminder of the transitory nature of the human condition. Birth and death were simply part and parcel of village life and the wider world. He made this point with exceptional eloquence the very week of poor Mia's tragic passing in one of his sermons. In fact, Tibbs spoke so well and with such conviction and humility on the subject that Mark Tanner quoted some of the Reverend's sermons on his CashSplash page. This caused a murmur of concern from Gemma, who felt that Mark Tanner would surely be sued for infringement of copyright. Luckily, the minister took Mark's intellectual theft in the spirit to which it had been meant—one of flattery and deference. The Reverend went on to discuss the point of plagiarism in his subsequent sermon, stating that the word of God was open and available to all. It had no copyright. Lift whatever you liked, and there would be no negative reckoning.

In effect, the village was, therefore, already well-versed in death, its speed, its logistical implications, its potential for public oratory, and its possibility for philosophical creativity and reflection. Only, to Julia, the death felt more immediate, more personal. She had been at the house the evening before. She had practically been ahead of the police getting there this very morning. In truth, Lady Hortishall horizontally vacating the Hall was a terrible shock.

Therefore, safely installed in Sal's café, Julia clutched her warm mug of sugary tea tight between both hands—as tight as a person pushed out of an aeroplane without a parachute might cling to a tailgate. This usually cool and collected woman, with a propensity for order and a belief that all would be well, was totally and utterly flummoxed.

'Was Her Ladyship dead?' Sal repeated her initial question after what had been an exorbitantly long pause.

'I'm not sure,' Julia managed eventually.

'Did you see an ambulance?' Artie wanted to know. The chalk menu board remained unwritten. The offerings for the day were undecided in all the commotion.

'The ambulance arrived just before I left,' Julia affirmed without offering anyone eye contact.

'And a stretcher?' Gemma said. 'Was the body covered or uncovered?' Gemma was always one for fine detail.

Julia scanned her mind back, but there seemed to be bits missing, reluctant to surface. 'I don't think I saw a stretcher. At least, not when I was there.'

'No stretcher.' Sal echoed thoughtfully.

'And you say you saw all the gardeners leave last night together?' Gwyn asked, with a narrowing of her eyes.

The woman seriously did fancy herself as a Miss Marple. Julia couldn't for the life of her see why the presence of the gardeners would have any relevance whatsoever to anything, but she nodded in affirmation anyway. 'Every last one,' she said. 'I closed the gate after them myself.'

For some reason, this caused an odd silence to descend. Strange, because the small café was a hive of activity. There seemed to be a plant swap going on. People traded perennials in advance of the open garden event always held in November. These were the things that village life should be made of. Instantly, Julia wished she hadn't mentioned the stretcher or the gate because on voicing these plot points in the demise of Her Ladyship, it felt as if there were some greater design here than mere misfortune—a design larger than slipping a blue envelope through the letter box of the front door and onto a mat, which might not exist.

Mark Tanner broke the silence, clearing his throat in an irritated manner. 'This is just the bare facts. We need more.'

Julia felt she had already said more than enough. Luckily, Carris took over.

'I could take the Bongo for a spin?' She offered helpfully. 'I could make up some excuse.' The young library assistant's forehead creased in consternation. 'What could I say I was up to?' she whispered, more to herself than anyone else. No one else was interested anyway besides, the café was getting very crowded. There was barely enough room to breathe, let alone think.

'I knew there was a problem.' Blythe Nithercote said sagely. 'My bees have been acting odd all week.'

Nobody paid any attention to Blythe since Blythe's bees were always "acting odd."

'We need to get that Mumblings boy in here.' Silas said. Silas had been saying this for the past week. Truth be known, Silas wanted to chew PC Mumblings' ear off about the common debacle. No surprise, since the unfortunate Silas Mariner was about to be marooned, and despite what his name might imply, being marooned was not in his nature. The man had no nautical connections.

'Sorry,' Des said, pushing open the door and blustering in with his post bag still on his shoulder. 'Did I miss something?'

'Her Ladyship is dead.' Ruth said, flicking back her hair with a dramatic flounce.

'And we're in a bit of a quandary.' Marsha Wallace interjected. She'd taken time out from Reece's office but knew she'd have to be back soon and was eager for answers. 'We need PC Mumblings to give us the low-down,' she said eagerly. No doubt this was a deduction arrived at effortlessly. Marsha's logical mind had surely been developed over many mind-numbing years dedicated to organising and collating Reece's filing system. Yet Julia noticed the woman looked a little flushed at the mention of the policeman. Unusually, no one contradicted her. PC Mumblings was not a popular man. Silence fell once again. For the first time in his life, it would appear that the presence of Gary Mumblings was wanted, yet was curiously absent.

'The alarm.' Des said, his eyes lighting up in delight. 'We could set the library alarm off. PC Mumblings will have to investigate.'

Gemma smiled, looking more than satisfied. 'And, since it's perfectly possible that we would all be in the library at the same time.'

'With it being a public space.' Carris offered helpfully.

'It's absolutely valid...' Gemma continued. 'To give him the third degree.'

12

THE LIBRARY

It wasn't what Julia would describe as a comfortable experience. It wasn't every day that the sole purpose of an activity was to set off a loud, penetrating commotion in order to attract the attention of the law. Not that it didn't happen, but it was a very different experience for your Bruce Willis types in such Christmas classics as Die Hard. For a precision operation, a lone wolf approach often works well. Entering one's place of work with an entire village behind you is not easy. The "entire village" was, of course, an exaggeration. It was a school day.

'Can't you turn it down?' Silas said. The alarm was playing havoc with his tinnitus. Many a member of the community found themselves tearing out their hearing aids in horror.

'I'm afraid...' Julia shouted above the noise as they plundered through the narrow doorway, a fair few bodies falling into a heap just the other side of the quick bookshelf, 'it's a one-setting kind of a thing.'

'Blast,' Geoff said, pulling himself back up in a surprisingly nimble fashion. 'I should have filmed that.' But as was always the case with Geoff, he found himself just the wrong side of too late.

Carris looked confused. 'Do we have to keep the thing on?'

Julia nodded, her face scrunched and tortured at the acoustic assault. 'If we don't keep it on, Mumblings will think we just messed up.'

'We could sing,' Salvatori suggested. 'I'm pretty sure that's an E-sharp in there somewhere.' He cleared his throat and gave a quick, suitably impressive demonstration. A couple of the choir joined in, but since the refrain was not taken up unanimously, the scheme soon fell flat.

'I could wheel out my organ.' Beatrice said helpfully. 'It would only take me a tick to nip back and hook it onto the trailer.'

Gemma shot Beatrice an irritated look; the woman was always trying to push her organ in anywhere it had no place to be. 'You can't park it on the road. You'd have to bring it in, and I seriously can't see that it would make anything any better,' she said, and a couple of people nodded.

'There is the disabled spot,' Mrs Talbot offered, at which Gemma looked as though she might happily throttle the woman.

The stress of the morning, the overcrowding and the persistence of the alarm were all proving too much. Julia took the manager's decision and switched the thing off. Peace descended. Ruth Silverling stopped dancing like a dervish, her skirts flying and took time to inhale. Curtis was heard to let out a sigh.

Even Mrs Talbot reached out one withered brown hand, resting it gently on Gemma's shoulder. 'I'm sorry, dear. I forgot. I don't have the right to be giving out that space, seeing as I don't actually have the badge. Yet, even if my eyelids are remarkably sore this morning.' With that, the old woman flitted those "sore" eyes of hers ceiling ward as though trying to recall the words of the book she'd been given. 'Most likely, it's hay fever,' she added very reasonably.

Gemma took in a deep breath and, no doubt, drew on the advice she had also gleaned from a recent engagement with literary sources, such as the universally applauded Dr Smart-Alec's *How to Avoid Alienating Friends and Family*. Gemma replied in a tone that was sweet and genuine enough at least to pass. 'Many people find a daily dose of antihistamine very helpful this time of year.'

A collective sigh of relief passed over the crowded library. The shoulders of all those present dropped the hackles fell away.

It was only then that Julia noticed all was not, in fact, well; there was an outsider in their midst. The library was filled to bursting with all the usual suspects, but at some point in time, before the community fell through the door, dancing around the room, complaining about the noise, and making their own peace, a stranger had struck through the chaos. Julia might have been a woman recovering from shock, a person buoyed up from Sal's sugared tea and a leader - in what was fast becoming known as 'the village alarm honey-trap'—a rouse designed to entice PC Mumblings down from the hill - but Julia was, at heart, a consummate professional, a long-time library manager, and a woman who had dedicated her entire working life to the distribution of free books.

'Lovely,' she said, in an attitude of genuine and unconditional warmth, eyeing the face of the stranger with a welcoming middle-distant gaze, full of smiles. 'Are you a member, sir? Registration only takes a second.' Nobody saw her reach the ballpoint, yet there it was in her hand with the slim A5 membership card favoured by the Suffolk service.

As soon as the man's presence was highlighted, the library fell into a different kind of silence than the one they had achieved by the switching off of the alarm. That particular silence had reflected relief—the combined relief of all present. This current silence was driven by curiosity. The man was not unusual looking, although he was sporting an M&S navy suit from their Italian slim fit collection, according to Ruth Silverling, who had never been known to be wrong on the point of fashion. His hair was dark but not black. His eyes appeared to have no colour, reflecting only the dominant features of the room. You could not describe him as a tall man, but to call him short would be misleading. In fact, if it had not been for the commotion, there was a strong likelihood that the man would not have been noticed.

'Mr Perkins,' Carris said, clutching her chest in an attitude of adoration, as she shifted her position in the room in order to get a closer inspection of the man's ring finger—a finger which happened to be empty. It did not go unnoticed that, on seeing the absence of matrimonial labelling, the young library assistant let out a sigh.

Although there had been a lot of talk in the library community and a couple of photofit-style images circling on the covert, under-the-radar Librarian Liberation Facebook page, there were no actual photographs of Mr Perkins—the new regional manager. Not for the first time, Julia couldn't help but be impressed by Carris' ability to deduce information from a position of want rather than one of knowledge. No doubt she was sizing Perkins up for the Bongo and relieved to see the man could easily fit. The vehicle even had a hanging closet, so it would be no problem to accommodate the suit.

'The sign-up is necessary, sir,' Julia said, and it was noted there was a pause between the "necessary" and the "sir." No one was quite sure what the purpose was by this, in itself may have been Julia's intent.

'Will you be borrowing with us today,' Julia said. 'I'm sorry I'm not yet aware of your reading habits, but if you point me in the right direction, I'm sure I will be able to pull something from the shelves.'

'Thank you,' the man said.

He was affirmative, Julia felt and knew his manners. A formal introduction would have been nice, but Mr Perkins had wandered into her space. It was, therefore, her position to host. 'Not at all,' she said, adding a smile.

He drew in a breath. 'I shan't be borrowing today. I have found that since taking on my latest promotion, my TBR list is taking over.'

Julia smiled. However, some of the other members of the community looked blank, unfamiliar as they were with the technical abbreviations used in the book-borrowing community. TBR, or To Be Read, most likely went over most of their heads. Blythe Nithercote even took a step away. Believing in the healing powers of bees, Blythe had never been vaccinated for anything—a habit which always made her wary of outsiders.

'In fact,' Mr Perkins said, 'this is not a social call.'

Julia hadn't thought for one moment that it would be, but poor Carris let out a whimper.

'I'm here to check on the whereabouts of the self-service machine.'

Fortunately, the machine was now completely covered by the artistic endeavours of the preschoolers. There was not an inch of metal showing.

Julia knew that in a small village, one should never

speak an untruth—not if you wanted to be trusted. She must choose her words carefully and answer the man with a question. 'Has the rollout been completed?'

He nodded, drawing in his thin lips a little before making his reply. 'Almost.'

An "almost" was all that Julia needed. 'Right,' she responded—a word which, of course, means absolutely nothing.

'I must say...' Perkins glanced around him at the burgeoning room and the compliant locals who, at the mention of the self-service machine, had each pulled a book from a shelf and were busying themselves in the pursuit of what appeared to be reading. 'Yes,' Perkins gave a satisfied nod. 'I must say, I'm impressed by your footfall.'

Although Julia disliked reducing the entire isolated rural community to a bleep on a counting machine, she was all too aware of the importance of choosing one's battles. 'We're very popular,' she admitted, fighting an irresistible urge to glance over at the IT section with its large circular clock hanging on the wall. In truth, she had so many questions. How long had the alarm been off? Was Mumblings on the way? What would the regional manager think if the police arrived and the community began its impromptu interrogation of the police constable on library property? Was cross-pollination of information via county employees even allowed? Luckily, Prue Purlington saved the day with a pair of scissors and an invisible seam. As Perkins had been talking, otherwise engaged with Julia, Prue had unpicked the back of his smart jacket with a seam ripper. This particular ability had won her many awards in national and local competitions when she toured the county shows with a group of sheep-shearing enthusiasts. All these talents were well known; however, everyone gathered in the library, pretending to read, was seriously impressed by Prue's acting abilities.

'Oh dear,' she said in a seemingly spontaneous manner. 'Your jacket's ripped, young man.'

In truth, he wasn't young, but people always think of knitters as being ancient beings, creatures of stoicism and wisdom, a misconception she often used to her advantage. 'If you come to my woollen shop,' Prue continued. 'I've got just the right shade of thread to match that navy. I can do you some invisible stitching in next to no time.'

Perkins looked a little taken aback, and for more than a moment, a weighty silence descended on the library; no one was quite sure of how this would all play out. Prue, however, was undeterred. 'I've won medals for just this situation,' she said brightly, lifting down a copy of *Knit-Wit's Quarterly* from the magazine rack and opening it to the relevant page. When the man hesitated, yet again, Prue reached for the rack. This time, it was *The Quirky Quilter* she was offering up as evidence, a publication in which Prue's small, classified ad detailing her sought-after abilities was seen by people in the same predicament all over the country.

Perkins couldn't argue with the written endorsements. He was, he said, aghast at the suit's lack of quality. As Ruth had so rightly predicted, the item was from the M&S slim-fit Italian collection. He'd only had it three years and had kept the article in question on rotation with a dogtooth suit of the same style. Which meant the navy number could only have been worn a total of five hundred and forty-seven times. His shifts were barely ever over eight hours long since the council didn't pay overtime. M&S were normally known for their quality—hence the shock. Prue secreted her scissors back in her pocket as many in the library also voiced their consternation. Consternation Voicing was a bit of a local occupation; it could go on for hours, especially when there was a summer solstice in the mix. However, on this occasion, it was clearly in most people's interests if the consternation was cut short with there being more pressing items to be dealt with. Not surprisingly, all those (apart from Carris) were pleased to see the back of the man. And, as it turned out, not a moment too soon.

For only minutes after Prue and Perkins had cleared the road, Gary Mumblings appeared in his Panda. He drove straight into the disabled space. Julia rested a hand on Gemma's arm—this was not the time. Pierre was sent out the backway to grab a few fresh baked croissants from his restaurant on the green. Sal whipped over to the Snippy Biscuit to pick up a chai latte—Gary's favourite, whilst Carris was sent out to the Spa to get the man a pack of gum —for old time's sake. In short, all bases were covered. The tables had shifted. Gary was normally someone you'd pay a gang of ne'er-do-wells to have abducted, but now the whole village could barely get enough of the constable with his large lips that they hoped would start flapping.

13

PC MUMBLINGS

'Natural causes,' Gary announced after the final flakes of his third croissant fell to the lap of his grey trousers.

Julia couldn't help but wonder if Gary would be having a bad case of *natural causes* if the man didn't slow down on the flaky pastry front. He had kept them guessing for far longer than was strictly necessary. It was, therefore, inevitable that after the well-nourished police constable had spilt his significantly under-sauced beans, a wave of disappointment bordering on irritation washed over the gathered. It wasn't just that there were no juicy details to be gleaned on the morning's events; Gary clearly had no clue whatsoever as to what would be happening to the common in the wake of Her Ladyship's demise. Of course, that had not deterred the wiseacre Mumblings from dropping numerous pointed insinuations to the contrary, such as the perennially madding catchall "I'm afraid I'm not at liberty to divulge that kind of information" or the all-time favourite cop-out "I must respect the privacy of the individuals involved,"—a catchphrase which had clearly been misappropriated by the force since the boys/girls & others in blue, frequently arrived in an attention-grabbing blaze of sirens. To finish it all off, there was the downright childish, “Now that would be telling.” The man was so on-script that nobody bothered pointing out the blindingly obvious; those directly involved with the common debacle couldn’t give a fig about privacy anymore; the large literal and metaphorical hedge which surrounded their lives, and the whims of the recently deceased aristocracy, had to come down.

In short, by the time PC Mumblings had chewed his last mouthful, the entire library was beyond frustrated, past the point of bewildered, and was resting somewhere in the passive predicament of sagging-shouldered disappointment —a state which manifested itself not just in shoulders, sighs and irritated frowns but by a collective and comprehensive kinaesthetic leaching. The only things which kept the community going appeared to be Megan Keeble’s kind offer of cuttings for the garden and Sal’s hot coffees served from a flask. But the light had even gone out of those small kindnesses. The library appeared to have all the energy of a deflated balloon. Regi Brewhound felt miffed since the “impromptu” meeting hadn’t been held in the Dog and Duck. He could have sold a barrel worth of cider and a good few packets of crisps, not to mention the pork scratchings, which was always a favourite and had a significant profit margin–being only pig fat with a randomly attached stringy bit of hoggish chin hair. The movement of merchandise would have been infinitely possible—if there had only been more planning on the venue front.

Des felt exhausted; he’d been on the early shift that morning for his postal round, and even before things had kicked off at the Snippy Biscuit, Des had already had himself an odyssey of experiences—he had tackled angry dogs with snarling jowls, encountered ethereal women with their faces still in sleep masks and their heads encased in hydra crowns of rollers and not to mention an unfortunate attack on his van by a pheasant with a death wish or, indeed, the personal irritation of a shoelace that would not stay tied. In the wake of Mumblings' delivery, poor Des became acutely aware of one sad fact—he missed his bed.

Although, perhaps it was Mark Tanner who felt the crush of disappointment after the Mumblings' announcement most profoundly. With all the commotion, Mark had neglected to learn how to TikTok. It was common knowledge that the man's CashSplash page was not going well. It was also common knowledge that, being a person with not a lot of time left, Mark could not afford to take time out. So, when Megan Keeble announced she had to get back to her cats, a collective sigh of relief passed over the gathered; everyone knew that the meeting had finally come to a close. Nobody had to "get back to their cats." Being a cat-loving community, most of the village had read *Not Giving a Furball*, and *Zen and the Art of Cat Apathy*. Everyone could spot Megan's excuse was simply a case of fobbing off, and so, as was often the case when people were feeling foolish, the crowd disappeared in a matter of seconds.

'I don't really know what they all expected,' Carris said, removing the gum from under the IT table where Gary had stuck it. 'When there's a death, people seem to want all the gory details.' There was a philosophical note to the young library assistant's enquiry as she wrapped the gum in one of the tissues, which Julia always kept on her desk in case of emotional breakdowns. They were as standard in most libraries as fire extinguishers. They were a necessity since some of the Romance titles carried by the library system contained provocative prose, and, contrary to popular belief, it isn't just Scouts who feel the need to be prepared. 'Why is that, Julia?' Carris asked thoughtfully, letting the small tissue package drop into the non-recycling. 'What do people want out of a blow-by-blow account of a death?'

Julia wasn't sure if she was unable or unwilling to answer this question. No doubt the Reverend Tibbs would hold more than a few views on the subject matter. This seemed to be more in his ballpark. Therefore, it was a shame that he'd hurried away so promptly with the others, muttering something about his current chronic shortage of surplices and the advantages of the new non-chemical bleaching agents that could be purchased directly from Amazon and put on next-day delivery if identified in the purchasing options as an "add-on item."

Perhaps, Julia felt, discussing the deceased had a kind of inverse outcome. It made the living feel more alive. As if they, too, had been standing above the dark mouth of the abyss, tottering in the mercurial currents of chance. And yet, praise be, they had managed to maintain their footing. Whatever the nugget of wisdom was, that was certainly lying somewhere at the hardcore end of this existential reflection, Julia didn't bother to reply. No. Unlike the others, Julia had not been disappointed by the painfully thin and sketchy details offered by the police constable. Instead, the library manager had found herself wallowing in an overwhelming sense of relief. Gary hadn't even mentioned the letter on the doorstep. Perhaps Her Ladyship had burned the letter late last night whilst she was still breathing and maintaining a regular heartbeat. Perhaps she buried the thing in ashes via the large open grate of the main Hall. Although a wonderful image, Julia quickly realised that this was unlikely. Being June, nobody was lighting fires. Besides, the gesture would have been overdramatic and detrimental to the planet. Julia's mildly threatening handwritten letter would most likely be in the waste disposal, heading off to be buried in a landfill with Gary's gum, or perhaps it had gone in the recycling and therefore, would be repurposed into something beautiful and functional like notebooks for children in inner city areas. Julia liked this thought. It was the kind of thought that warmed the heart, and for a moment, she allowed herself a little time to bask in its reflection. All would be well. The problem had been avoided, and miraculously, the small rural community had also dodged the bullet that could have been Mr Perkins.

'I suppose,' Julia said, stretching out her body and releasing her shoulders, which she had found were becoming increasingly tight of late. 'One of us better go and rescue the regional manager.' It was common knowledge that you only had to walk into Prue's shop for a pair of scissors for the woman to engage you in some kind of human loom-making activity. There was always a fresh skein of yarn waiting to be balled, and as everybody knew, the process of yarn balling needed four willing hands. 'You can go if you like,' Julia said kindly, realising that this might be Carris' only chance for a more intimate encounter with the man from head office. Library conventions were always very crowded, and the ratio of available men to women was ridiculously low. If Perkins floated himself on the open market, Carris would not get a look-in.

Therefore, Julia's plan seemed sound, but to her surprise, young Carris only crinkled her nose.

'I don't know Julia. There's a lot of books to be stamped back in.' She glanced around the library, which was, in fact, despite the sudden influx of footfall, almost back to its regular glory.

Julia paused for thought before replying, realising there

could well be other factors at play here and felt that a little more insight might well be a good thing. 'Am I sensing, Carris,' the library manager said, drawing out her words, giving the recipient the time to fully focus, 'that you've cooled slightly to our Mr Perkins?'

'Oh, Julia,' Carris flopped her buttocks down on the wheeled desk chair and proceeded to swivel idly side to side with all the direction of a disgruntled teenager. The chair let out small squeaks of metal every time it swung itself from right to left. 'I know that a woman shouldn't judge...'

Julia nodded sagely, aware that there was a "but" on its way.

Carris sighed. 'I have always had a problem with dogtooth suits.'

Julia looked confused. 'The man was in navy?'

'Oh,' Carris threw her arms into a wide, dramatic, dismissive gesticulation. It was a movement she was especially fond of when feeling flummoxed, overwhelmed, or in need of a frozen margarita. 'He mentioned he had a dogtooth at home.'

'Ah.' Julia said, knowing that something needed to be said at this juncture and that a short, non-committal sound might be better than defining the tone of the conversation with a verb, noun or adjective.

'It made me realise,' Carris continued, 'that age is important. That...' She paused, taking a moment to steal herself, 'I shouldn't be throwing myself away on the first regional manager who just so happens to walk through our door in search of his self-service machine.'

'Very wise,' Julia concurred.

Carris exhaled a thin stream of satisfied air before resting her head thoughtfully to one side. 'Maybe I don't need someone in the library system.'

Julia couldn't help but agree. Inter-library relationships were always frowned upon. However, in order not to break the flow, she simply nodded, letting out a small, barely audible 'ah.'

'Just imagine if we had children,' Carris said, her face lengthening into horse-style proportions at the sheer affront of the speculation. 'They'd never get their heads out of a book, and...' she paused, clearly thinking this all over in the moment, with a logical precision alien to the young library assistant. 'I have to think about these things,' she admitted sagely. Her features switched in an instant from elongated equine and shocked to pinched as a sour citrus and worried. 'I'm running out of time on the child-rearing front. And...' She paused, her little body seeming to straighten. Her posture unfolded as steadily as a repurposed six-by-six sheet of origami. Suddenly, the woman's eyes, which were so often befuddled and confused, switched to a more inspirational attitude of misty and glazed. She offered up the sort of eyes that attracted a strongly commercial, galvanising soundtrack on a par with the Vangelis' motivational anthem for *Chariots of Fire*—a song which was almost impossible to hear without wanting to run in slow-mo with the wind in one's hair. 'Can you imagine,' Carris said, her voice filled with rare passion, 'the joy of having a baby in the Bongo?'

Julia could not, but having worked in the library system for so long, she was a woman who knew not to comment on the dreams of others.

'I'm worth more,' Carris said decisively. 'I deserve to be loved,' she continued with shocking certainty.

That was when Julia realised with a heavy heart that it was most likely Carris who had been plundering the self-help shelves. No doubt she'd been over-ordering on the dynamic stock, purchasing titles on the quiet and hoarding any books that happened to come out of circulation and go into the for-sale, battered, broken and unwanted bucket by the door. This might even be why her Bongo was going slower—Carris had been weighing the vehicle down. She was cramming its carefully crafted cupboards not with digestives, powdered milk and pot noodles but with goal-orientated titles from the bargain book box. But none of that mattered. Not now.

'Right-oh,' Julia said brightly, not wanting to get into any kind of discussion with a misty-eyed Carris, especially when they should be closing up the library in less than an hour. 'I'll go rescue him myself.'

'Wonderful,' Carris said, although Julia wasn't convinced that Carris had even heard. The woman was clearly manifesting at that very moment. Therefore, no personal explanation was needed, or indeed, possible.

~

FORTUNATELY, when Julia arrived at the Old Yarn, Perkins had already vacated the shop. Not everyone was delighted by this. Prue certainly wasn't happy. She had kept her part of the deal, sewing the man's jacket with a finesse that Cinderella's godmother would have been impressed by, but Perkins proved to be a fidget. As soon as he'd got what he wanted, he'd been unwilling to offer any assistance and had been out of the door without even paying for the price of the cotton. Prue had very clearly had to break open a new bobbin. So now she was not only short on time but also on pocket. The shop owner had never liked people with an acute lack of altruism and, therefore, she felt that perhaps Carris had secured herself a lucky escape. Despite the curiously satisfying ability to mount herself on a high horse,

Prue was not happy. Perkins had put her way behind on her to-do list. She wished she'd never met the man.

Julia didn't bother to remind Prue that it was actually the wool saleswoman who had sabotaged the regional manager's jacket in the first place, or that the relationship with Perkins and Carris had only ever been happening in Carris' small, bird-like head.

However, credit where credit was due—Prue had come to the rescue of the community by distracting an unwanted guest. It was almost closing, and the woman still had two skeins of mohair to ball, which was always a tricky operation since the super soft strings of wool were liable to melt away in the fingers when pulled too hard. So, Julia had done the decent thing. She had sat for a while, hands extended out in front of her like a forklift, while Prue rolled. And as Julia sat peacefully in the wool shop, with its faint aromas of lanolin mixed with the different dyes - turmeric for the yellows, the sweet smell of cochineal for the reds, and the herbal odours of the madder plant, which was so popular for its pretty pinks - Julia had felt a sense of peace descending, watching the yarn wind from her hands into Prue's constantly moving ball. The day was almost over. Most of the crises that had reared seemed to have been avoided. Tomorrow, Julia would be free to get on with the main issue —the one which was pressing on her soul like the weight of an unwanted corset: the whereabouts of the missing books. She would not let the matter drop. Even if Her Ladyship had literally and unwittingly done that very thing. If Julia could just find out the whereabouts of the missing volumes, surely she would be able to wrangle them back to the library.

Perhaps, it could be argued, that Lady Hortishall was already suffering from diminished responsibilities before she breathed her last. After all, the woman had a terminal case of natural causes about to descend. This would surely have affected her capacity for decision-making. Julia decided to make a note on this very subject, one that she could bring up with Dr Carter as soon as was humanly possible. The library manager would need to make a case to the courts. As Julia sat in the warmth of the shop, basking in the sweet smells, watching as the wool wound continually from her hands, those books could even be heading to the auction houses now or setting sail on ships, never to be seen again. The thought made a small tear of frustration form in the library manager's tired eyes. She suddenly felt very old for such a bit of fight. Thankfully, for the moment, she had found herself in a brief pocket of peace.

As the wool wound and the clock ticked, Julia gazed out of the window at the small rural community of which she had become so fond of: its narrow streets, its high curbs and its tottering medieval houses that seemed to lean on each other as though offering support. If you took one out, perhaps the whole village would fall. And just as Julia was dwelling on the pleasant possibility of what she would have for tea and wishing, although she knew the irony of it, that there would be a cat on her hearth waiting to welcome her home for the evening, her heart seemed to drop. She leaned forward in her chair, causing Prue's balling to wobble in her wake. Sadly, however, the action was unavoidable, the movement involuntary, for who should Julia spy coming out of Reece's office but PC Gary Mumblings. The man clearly had more beans than he was letting slip. Why else would he be visiting Reece? But all was not lost. Paying a short, sharp visit to the solicitor herself might give Julia the upper hand on the whereabouts of the books and the state of the common.

'Prue,' Julia said decisively. 'You're going to need to use

some chair legs instead of my hands for the balling or improvise.' Julia glanced around the shop, catching sight of a crate with flower cuttings. 'Or perhaps that crate? Although I would love to stay, I myself have important business that needs sorting.'

14

REECE

If Prue was disappointed, she managed to keep it to herself. Most people liked Julia. She had an agreeable nature and was free with her favours. Besides, Prue was bored now and itching to close up the shop. Trade had been slow, and the wool enthusiast had promised herself an evening of Fair Isle colour work using the controversial geometric blocking of brown and green, which, as every knitter knew, was a combination that should never be seen. Prue, however, was non-conformist by nature, and, therefore, the thought of an evening engaged in an activity with a mildly subversive inclination. As soon as Julia walked out of the door, Prue turned the welcome sign hanging on the glass shop door from "Open for yarn" to "Wound down."

The door next to the woollen shop was always closed. One had to ring or knock to gain entrance. Since the doorbell was unpredictable, Julia found herself banging, once again, on the door to the solicitors. She gave a short series of raps before waiting to see if there was movement inside, and then she banged again. Luckily, it wasn't long before Julia heard the light step of feet on the staircase in the hall, and the heavy door was pulled open.

'Julia,' Marsha said brightly, though there was a tiredness to her attitude that Julia couldn't quite place.

'I just wanted to have a quick word with Reece.' Julia said, trying to push forward.

'Oh, I'm so sorry,' Marsha said, not sounding sorry at all. 'I'm afraid you've missed him.'

This was odd; Julia's forehead crosshatched into a frown. 'Not in?'

'No,' Marsha repeated, glancing up and down the road in a furtive fashion. 'He won't be back now.'

'Right. I think I might pay him a house call.' Julia said, more to herself than Marsha. 'This needs to be sorted soon.'

Marsha smiled a little officiously. 'Best to give him a call before you go. It's his night for the ramblers, and I'm not sure what time they set off.'

'Good idea,' Julia reached into her small blue bag for her phone. 'Always good to plan ahead.' Only there were no bars on the small device. 'Blast,' she said, genuinely disappointed. 'I've got no signal,' she glanced at her wristwatch, 'And the library will be closed by now. I wonder, could I borrow your line, Marsha?'

At this, the strangest thing happened. Marsha's features seemed to pale.

'Marsha?'

The woman looked decidedly awkward.

'Are you all right?'

The woman pulled in a deep breath before answering. 'I'm so sorry, Julia. I've been told not to let you in.'

'Me?' Puzzled, Julia clutched her hand to her chest.

'Well, not you personally,' Marsha said, looking decidedly rattled. 'Anyone. You see, we've got a bit of a problem.'

Her voice suddenly sounded more assured, as if she had found her way. 'In the office, a problem in the office. Reece has said no one can come in for the foreseeable.'

Julia's eyes narrowed. 'What about PC Mumblings then?'

Instantly, Marsha's face flushed into a crimson that any woollen provider would have been proud to stock on their shelves.

'I just saw Gary...'

'Shh', Marsha said urgently. 'All right, Julia, you win.' Marsha glanced once again up and down the road. 'But you can't go in Reece's office, and it's only to use the phone.

As Julia climbed the too-narrow wooden staircase behind Marsha's large rump, wrapped in its habitual A-line skirt, the library manager couldn't understand what was going on. Why wouldn't Reece want any of the villagers in his office? They were his main stock in trade. Perhaps he had grown weary over the constant questions about the common. Perhaps it was understandable that the solicitor had chosen to keep a low profile.

The nature of the Mumblings visit became apparent as soon as Marsha led Julia through the door and into the reception area. There was the odd ylang-ylang, sandalwood and patchouli. The cogs in Julia's head clicked into place, for what was the book which Marsha had taken out only last week? *Aroma and Amore*. Mumblings had not been delivering news. All the patisseries he'd been scoffing had clearly made the man desire a little something for dessert. Anyone having Mumblings as a love interest was a thought which demanded a true paradigm shift. However, Julia was a person who prided herself on her tolerance for the romantic interests of others. Mumblings and Marsha were grown-ups. The constable had a penchant for desks. The secretary had one. No doubt, Mumblings' gum was, even now, drying out on the underside of Marsha's office furniture.

'Right, well,' Julia said awkwardly. 'I'll just phone Reece. Then I'll be out of your way.'

Marsha smiled sheepishly back; she clearly knew she'd been caught in the act of subterfuge—an uncomfortable position at the best of times. 'Here,' she said, 'handing Julia the buzzing handset.

Julia took it, almost wishing she didn't have to. She shouldn't be here. Talking to Reece could have waited surely till tomorrow. But it was too late now. She was on a path, and the only possibility was stepping forward.

'I'll just...' she pressed the number in quickly. The tones sounded oddly reassuring. Soon, she would be talking to Reece and could forget about her little discovery.

'I'm so sorry I was brusque earlier,' Marsha said sweetly. 'It's just...' she sighed. 'The lack of space has been getting me down.' She gesticulated towards Reece's office. 'Hopefully, they'll be gone soon.'

'Exactly.' Julia said, not understanding what she was referring to but enjoying the tone of normality, which appeared to be returning.

'I mean, we've had them here for months,' Marsha said, her voice sounding brittle and exhausted. 'I can barely get a duster around.'

'Have you tried the ostrich feather one they sell in the Handy Man?' Julia asked brightly. The dusters really were a treat.

'No,' Marsha said. 'I'll do that. That would at least help me do the spines,' she said lightly, looking over to Reece's office. Julia followed her gaze, and then poor Julia's world came tumbling down.

'Hello, Reece's residence?' said the voice on the other

end of the phone, but Julia could offer nothing back. She was truly dumbfounded because Reece's office had all the appearance of an Irish landmark and not St Patrick's Cathedral. No. This was way more Giant's Causeway. Because stacked all over Reece's room, with barely the space for a foot, were towers of books with spines embossed with gold. These were the Hortishall books.

'Hello?' came the small voice from what seemed like a different world.

'Julia?' Marsha said, concerned. 'Are you alright?'

But Julia could barely catch her breath, and then there was the thundering noise in her ears. Was it her heart? Were natural causes catching her up? What was the meaning of all of this? Then it all became clear, the thundering was not, in fact, her poor heart. No. The thundering belonged to PC Mumblings.

'Gary?' Marsha said, confused.

'PC Mumblings,' Gary said in correction, looking as bewildered as a ferret caught in the headlights of a combine harvester. Everything was wrong.

'It doesn't matter, Gary.' Marsha said, tears pricking her eyes. 'Julia knows. I shouldn't have borrowed that book.'

In retrospect, of course, it all seemed obvious. Marsha was a woman who liked to let those seeking justice in. It was part of her very being.

'I signed an NDA,' Julia said reassuringly. 'I'm not at liberty to discuss your borrowing habits, Marsha.' In truth, the illicit affair seemed to be beside the point; Julia didn't care. She didn't care about Marsha or Gary or the terrible waste of essential oils on a romance which literally sent shivers down her spine. No, Julia felt betrayed by her friend, Reece. What were the books doing in his office? According to Marsha, they had been there for months. Why wouldn't he have said?

'It's all out,' Marsha said resolutely, still talking about her romantic inclination and totally unaware that Julia was on a completely different track. 'Now Julia knows, Gary, we should probably tell your mother.'

A look of utter panic washed over Gary's face. His features bleached paler than the pristine leaves of a hot-off-the-press paperback. However, if this was surprising, what came next wholeheartedly floored and flabbergasted the poor library manager.

15

INCARCERATION

Julia had not expected to find herself incarcerated. At first, she had thought that this was simply an overreaction connected to her recently acquired knowledge of the illicit affair happening most afternoons directly above The Old Yarn. Gary had always had a curious relationship with his mother and, therefore, would not want Marsha pressuring him into going public regarding his passions. It was understandable since, by their very nature, clandestine rendezvous tended to be something people were keen to keep quiet. Only for PC Mumblings, there was an additional concern—Gary wouldn't want people to think of himself as merely human. Ironically, perhaps, if set against the views of the local solicitor in whose premises Gary had been bonking, since *human* was the very status that Reece had been so vociferously vocal about maintaining for himself. In point of fact, Reece had threatened legal action when local journalist Gareth had attempted to publish images in the Gazette. Pictures depicting Reece with a curiously elongated head. For clarity (and legal reasons), it must be admitted here that those images were clearly achieved through an unusual occurrence of natural light and an opportunistic serendipity on the part of the photographer. And it was beyond a doubt that this was where the matter of Reece, and any imagined abduction, should rest.

In short, and returning circuitously to the point in hand, PC Mumblings liked to project himself as a guardian of the county. He might not be wearing a cape, but he considered himself above the more primitive, baser aspects of the day-to-day nitty-gritty. It was clearly evident from the way he carried his chest, puffed out in front of his legs like a rooster, that as a man in uniform with a badge, a Panda and a truncheon, Mumblings believed he should not be seen to engage in the rough and tumble of existence or place himself willingly in a vulnerable position. And, of course, he shouldn't be dressed most afternoons in nothing but his socks and garters in a solicitor's office, with an amorous admirer who did indeed make the man vulnerable.

However, it did not take long for Julia to realise her mistake with reference to her own arrest. It had nothing to do with Gary, Marsha or the discovery of the semi-sordid fragrant romps. Julia's clarity came after the gentle but firm hand on the head as she lowered herself into the police car, shortly following the bit when they told her that anything she said could be used against her in evidence. Not long after, a cluster of people in uniforms offered her a single phone call, a cup of tea and a milk chocolate Hobnob with reduced sugar content, which was, quite frankly, ridiculous because everybody knew in situations involving police cars, sirens and handcuffs, along with a good solicitor (leaving Reece, thankfully, out of the equation) sugar was the one thing that was needed. Besides, who in their right mind would give a monkey's about watching one's weight when about to be locked in a cell and cruelly deprived access to their own personal biscuit tin—not everyone liked a Hobnob.

Of course, Julia could see that in the circumstances of the Hortishall tragedy, some kind of action had needed to be taken, for it would appear that Lady Hortishall's death was light-years away from *natural.* And unfortunately, but understandably, a logical connection had been made between Her Ladyship and the local librarian. Julia's letters had been found. All five of them had been pulled with latex gloves from the recycling. Their pages, unfortunately, were smeared with accidental encounters from substances which clearly should not have been placed anywhere near the clean rubbish litter. The letters were, therefore, not only a mockery of environmental policies but substantial evidence of ill will on the part of the librarian. To the police, they were, in fact, exactly what was needed. There was also the incriminating, uncharacteristic behaviour displayed by the library manager on the very morning that Her Ladyship's body had been discovered—Julia's silence in the Snippy Biscuit had not gone unnoticed, and in rewinding Julia's movements, the police soon arrived with the gardening team up at the Hall. With no encouragement needed, all of the white-wearing landscape contractors had testified that someone closely resembling a photofit picture of Julia had seemed extra keen to close the gate after them on the final evening of Her Ladyship's life. The horticulturists had assumed that "helpfulness" had been at the core of the library manager's motives. However, as the detective inspector handling the case informed them after their interviews, it was always wise to leave assumptions aside when investigating a murder. Perhaps all of the above could have been explained away, brushed under the Persian-style carpets that proliferated the Hall and slipped through the cracks of memory. But, sadly, and perhaps most significantly, the police were in possession of some highly incriminating CCTV footage—a videotape in which a near-retirement woman could be seen high in the arms of the wide cedar beside the Hall, leaning precariously out over the branches and placing a cat in the tree.

The detective was quick to link actions with purpose. Julia appeared to have motive by the bucket load, and it was soon clear that a failed promise for the transport and distribution of valuable books had become the catalyst for a heinous crime. The fact that Julia now knew where the said books were (languishing on the floor of Reece's office) was irrelevant. The murder was committed before the library manager's discovery of Reece's cruel betrayal. The investigating detective omitted the "cruel betrayal" part during his description since the stenographers employed by the law enforcement agency had never been enamoured by adjectives. But for Julia, the words Reece and betrayal were now forever linked.

~

It was not until the second day of Julia's confinement in her sparse, concrete cell that the much-maligned library manager received a visitor. Luckily, the solitary nature of those first few days of involuntary incarceration had not surprised the library manager. She had read enough regional crime bestsellers with quirky characters and unrealistic killings to know that the presiding DI of the unfamiliar market town in which Julia was currently languishing was most likely letting her stew—a constabulary device used by the force to glean confessions effectively. It was often used in conjunction with the good cop, bad cop routine, the one more day on the job trope, and the seasoned officer having a troubled past and (or) a host of intrusive family members with personal, political or verified clinical concerns. Having nothing whatsoever to confess, the "stewing" was, in effect, ineffective. Julia simply decided to take stock and practice her Tai chi.

However, she found herself more than a little disappointed when the much-awaited visitation, the thought of which had kept her sane when looking out of the small, high, barred window in her cell, happened to manifest itself in the form of Carris. In matters of murder, Carris, sadly, would probably be the last living creature that any being with an iota of innocence would want to see. Even Geoff would have been favourable. Since Julia might have been able to persuade the fledgling filmmaker to record her story, sell it to one of the popular streaming services and clear her name, which, as everyone with even an iota of sense now knew, was the only way to clear one's name, find yourself a partner, or have a brief but inspiring refit job on your house. In the twenty-first century, it was fast becoming impossible to get anything done unless you had a camera in your hand or craftily fixed to your lapel. Julia, of course, was only interested in the "clearing the name" part of the production slate. So, miraculously, it was conceivable that Geoff might, at last, have come into his own. But no. It would appear that Carris would be all that Julia was getting for the foreseeable.

'This is such a terrible muddle,' Carris blustered from the discomfort of her hard chair.

To the poor jailed Julia, "muddle" seemed badly balanced on the euphemistic side of the existential scales of experience, but she decided to let it go. It was, after all, the first time the library manager had spoken with a friendly face in any shape, form or function for forty-eight long hours, and therefore, Julia found herself unusually eager to give her larynx a smattering of exercise courtesy of a sympathetic audience. The "stewing" had obviously worked.

'I didn't touch the woman,' Julia said, irritated at having to continually protest her innocence, which was tensing every muscle in her body.

Carris shook her head emphatically. 'Of course, you didn't, Julia. We're all very concerned. It's most definitely a muskrat of justice.'

It would appear that poor Carris' brain was not keeping up. There were no muskrats involved in the predicament. The woman had mal-appropriated, as often happened in cases of custody. Carris had meant "miscarriage," which was exactly what this was.

'Eddy Bright's motivated the Parish Council.' Carris said breathily, as if she had been hurling herself physically through a process of redemption, which she was just about to describe. 'We're setting up a petition. We have one thousand signatures already. And Curtis...' She clutched at her chest as if the man truly were a hero. 'Curtis has been an absolute star. He's been in here every day arguing your innocence and explaining about the cat. That you were rescuing, not "placing" it. And that the creature had categorially never carried a camera in its collar. Never.' She shook her head emphatically. 'Even Geoff turned up at the station. He walked all the way, and you know how that standard issue independent filmmaker's leather jacket of his creaks. Oh Julia...' Carris looked at the library manager with starry eyes. 'You would have been so proud of the lad. He's been researching day and night in the library and turned up conclusive evidence from bona fide film producers who had found it impossible to work with cats. Kubrick said directing, and cats are absolutely an oxymoron, which means...'

'Yes, I know,' Julia said, trying not to sound snappy.

Oblivious, Carris rested her head thoughtfully on one side. 'Dolphins are apparently great for anything involving cinematography or spying. They're not camera-shy at all. Killer whales...' Carris rolled her eyes in grudging appreciation. 'Well, it turns out they're remarkable, but according to numerous verified sources, that was only if they feel in the mood, which is always difficult to ascertain. Also, they don't like filming in colour. Black and white or nothing. Which...' she grimaced, 'according to Geoff, is a film stock choice which can be seen as artsy and elitist.'

Julia didn't really need Carris to go into detail on the killer whale front. Everyone knew exactly what those large, grinning mammals were like on the non-conformity front. You only had to ask a seal. Not that you could, of course. In truth, life was one big joke to a killer whale. 'But cats.' Carris said, returning to her train of thought. 'Cats simply weren't interested in the filmmaking or any aspect of undercover surveillance. Even bit parts in fictional dramas are, apparently, a problem. The cat they used in *Alien*, Mr Jones,' she shook her head knowingly, 'apparently the bit where he runs off...' Carris leaned in across the table, dropping her voice to a whisper. 'That wasn't even scripted. In the official script written by Dan O'Bannon, Sigourney just gets away with the cat on her lap. They hop into that space pod thing with all the wires and the grey Hover-style gubbins and Sigourney, she simply pushes the thing into warp factor four. Smile on her face. No poor dentures and extra-terrestrial body fluids needed. But the cat wasn't compliant. Which I think,' Carris said, shooting her large open eyes to the ceiling as she assessed the merits of late eighties screenwriting. 'I think that was a good thing. It's everyone's favourite bit. So that whole franchise was quite clearly saved by one accidental happenstance.' Carris shrugged.

Her delight in the retelling of the intricacies of Ridley Scott's romp in space, turning the whole feature film into a parable of disguised blessings, came as no surprise to Julia. Along with self-help titles espousing the attraction of serendipity, Carris (like the rest of the village) was very partial to a little feline psychology.

'Sorry, Carris.' Julia rubbed the bridge of her nose in an attempt to stimulate her cerebral cortex. Sometimes, it was difficult to keep up with Carris' verbal wanderings. 'You may have lost me a little.' Having been without Carris for the last two days, the library manager had sadly forgotten the knack of listening to her assistant in order to extract any kind of sense.

'Sorry, sorry,' Carris' bottom lip pulled down into an upside-down smile. 'I'm getting off track. The gist is that cats are useless for filmmaking purposes. Completely ineffectual at gathering B roll or for stakeouts. Fiction or reality. They simply won't work. They're just not interested. So, therefore, you could not possibly have been "placing" the cat in the tree to spy on Her Ladyship's movements. Along with it being a bit strange,' Carris' brow furrowed into a frown, 'there would clearly be no point. Curtis is convinced they'll see sense eventually. He's been in everyday since you...' The woman stuttered. 'Since you received your...' She hesitated, 'exclusive invitation to the legal hospitality suit.'

Julia frowned, 'is that what you're calling it?'

Carris drew in a breath. 'Not to the people at head office. I told Perkins and all of the HR department that you were offered an all-expenses-paid holiday to a police-friendly neighbourhood.' Carris winced apologetically. 'It's going under a few different labels, but we thought that one was best for area management.' She glanced around her at the cold, concrete walls. 'Are the people being friendly?'

Julia shrugged, taking gratitude in the fact that having become such hot property, her case had been moved over to bigger guns than the local constabulary. PC Mumblings was not handling the investigations.

But all of this was beside the point. There was, in fact, only one thing that mattered. 'I need to get out,' she said plaintively.

'Oh, Julia,' Carris smiled sweetly. 'Of course you'll get out. We're all working on that now. Well, all apart from Reece.' She glanced down at her hands. 'He's keeping a low profile.'

It was understandable. However, there was something odd about Carris' reply, a degree of certainty about the impending freedom that Julia felt was misplaced. It seemed as if, to Carris, being locked up was a silly distraction, and of course, Julia would be walking away from it all soon. This made Julia nervous. 'I need to leave by the front door,' she said firmly. 'Not a tunnel, Carris.' She truly wished there wasn't the need to spell everything out, but with matters such as this and living in the type of community in which Julia had found herself embedded for the past thirty years, spelling it out seemed like the wisest course of action.

Carris laughed. 'Oh, Julia, you are a card. Don't you go worrying about anything.' The library assistant said blithely, reaching across the hard metal table and giving Julia's hand a quick squeeze. 'You'll be out in a tick. You just see if you're not.' Her eyes glinted as though there was a secret hidden somewhere behind them. 'And I promise,' she said, with an uncharacteristic degree of resolution, 'no tunnels.'

Julia could not help but feel even more disheartened.

Her long-time assistant, friend and side-kick seemed to be unnaturally unaware of the severity of the situation.

'In the meantime,' Carris continued. 'Des is being a power of strength. He comes in with me to open up every morning. He actually makes a detour just so he can help out. Then he drops in for a chat after his postal round, and he's always there for lock-up in the evening.' Carris pulled her shoulders into a shrug. 'I honestly don't know what we did before we had Des. He's a marvel, Julia. Simply a marvel.'

A sudden, awkward realisation hit Julia as sure as a ton of bricks flying hard and fast from a speeding freight train: she was superfluous, an irrelevant piece in the patchwork puzzle of village life. They were managing without her. They were, in fact, managing surprisingly well. Of all the things that the library manager had found upsetting in the past two years when most of this business had actually begun, the reality that she herself was so replaceable was, perhaps, the worst.

'Actually,' Carris' eyes sparkled despite the situation and the location. 'We've been sorting your retirement do.' Carris' eyes glistened brightly. 'Regi at the Dog and Duck has said we can have all the savoury food free, just imagine, as many quiches as you can eat! Pierre at *le Maison de Chien*, well, he's said he'll do us a bottomless tart.' She laughed, clapping her small hands together excitedly. 'Angie's already offered three barrels of cider, and not the watered-down type either.' She shot Julia a serious look. 'And, of course, the Young Wives and the WI are baking.' She grimaced slightly. It was common knowledge that things always got a bit competitive when both women's groups were involved. 'And...' Carris' ebullience seemed to take a step down. 'Blythe's offered her honey.' Carris shook her head sadly. A weight suddenly seemed to rest on the young, library assistant's shoulders. 'We couldn't get out of it. As usual...' Carris sighed, 'The woman put us in a sticky situation. I said to her couldn't you do a tray of honeycomb? Cut it up into squares to serve with the coffee. But oh no, you know what Blythe's like when she gets a bee in her bonnet.'

Julia did indeed know what Blythe was like. However, none of this made sense. 'Carris, I'm not going anywhere. I'm stuck. Completely stuck in here.'

'Oh Julia,' Carris laughed. 'You are daft sometimes.'

ONE OF THE most awful things about having been given a backstage pass to the legal symphony was that nobody tells you anything. You were simply left for vast tracks of time with worried thoughts and no access to a working kettle. As Julia stared every night at the ceiling from her hard bunk, she decided that when, and if, she were released, she would do something different with her life—the equivalent of Carris' Bongo, although not involving wheels, self-drive or cramped spaces. No, Julia would turn the page on a new chapter. She would live beside the sea or perhaps start her own private library. You didn't need to be a millionaire to collect books. Or maybe, then again, she wouldn't. Maybe she didn't want to be tied down. Julia realised, as she lay there, open-eyed and thinking, that the world was much bigger than many people gave it credit for, and now, rattling through her six decades on the planet, now would be a perfect time to explore. If only she could get out.

However, when the key eventually turned in the door, she did not initially assume that her newfound dream was actually kicking itself into action. There had been no whiff of freedom or talk of release—only cats, cameras and sea mammals. Even when she heard Gary's thick, rumbling voice telling her that all charges had been dropped and that she was free to go, Julia still didn't rush to the door. Most likely, she was suffering from Stockholm syndrome. A poorly named syndrome, if ever there was one, because it rarely happens in Stockholm anymore. The medical authorities there were hyper-vigilant about the possibility. Unfortunately, they were all still in Sweden. Nobody in Suffolk had a clue about anything like that. Phobias, manias, syndromes and anything psychosomatic were mainly thought to be curable (leaving vegetarians aside) with a bacon sandwich and a cup of tea. Yet, confusion kept Julia pinned to her cot for a full ten minutes after the door had been thrown back; the woman had been incarcerated for three days. Besides, you couldn't just kick a person out—there were questions that the ejected person had. A whole host of them, and these needed to be answered.

~

LUCKILY, it was Gary who drove Julia home. He'd become a little more subdued since the library manager's unfortunate arrest—less of a jobsworth and less full of himself.

'Tanner confessed,' Gary told her as they left the larger town, the one with the cell, behind.

Julia hadn't even asked, feeling that Gary was probably the wrong person for any kind of definitive clarification on any kind of mess-up. However, she felt thankful for the information. Although, she was more than a little surprised. 'Tanner! Mark?' The man of leylandii fame, naturism and one failed CashSplash page. 'Was it to do with the trees?'

'Trees?' Gary sounded confused.

'Jealousy over Her Ladyship's bush?'

Mumblings shook his head thoughtfully. 'Maybe. Partly. Not sure. He just confessed in full in his letter. He did mention the common—that he didn't like the way the Hortishalls had been literally lording it up over everyone for years and that the common had been a step too far.'

'Or not,' Julia added, since the bare bones of the ban had been that no one would be allowed to place one "step" on the land. 'What a total surprise.' Julia said, giving a slow, disbelieving shake of her head.

'Life's full of surprises,' Mumblings interjected dismissively, and Julia felt the man had missed the sheer scope of the unexpected which was at play here; Tanner was surely not the murdering kind. 'What is even more incredible,' Gary continued, twenty minutes later, flicking on the indicators and pulling up in front of Julia's sad, unlit home. 'Was his CashSplash page.'

Julia couldn't see how this was relevant, but she'd had enough for one evening. She was tired after her long incarceration, keen to switch on the kettle, run a bath, and place her heavy head upon her own lavender-infused pillow. Perhaps not even in that order. However, just to be sociable, she offered up an 'Oh?' anyway.

PC Mumblings nodded. 'Tanner got the full cash target for his Dignitas trip. Even had a little extra in his pocket for a toasted cheese sandwich and a packet of crisps on the way out.' Gary shook his head in astonishment. 'There was, of course, no need for anything on the way back.' PC Mumblings cleared his throat uncomfortably. Being a policeman, he didn't like to think of death in a sanitised way, with cheese sandwiches and refreshments. He was much more at home with a little more violence, pain and mess.

'I think it's very civilised,' said Julia, who had watched a documentary. 'Apparently, you get free chocolates in the clinic. All you can eat.'

'Milk or dark?' Gary asked.

This caused Julia to pause for thought. It was an interesting question and not one that the documentary filmmakers had unpacked. They'd just gone for the generic chocolate. But clearly, Gary was right. There was an important difference.

'It's Switzerland,' Julia said, as if that explained everything.

Gary continued to look mildly dumbfounded. 'He didn't mention the free chocolates in his letter.'

'Maybe he didn't know.' Julia liked to think that perhaps this was a pleasant surprise for the man after travelling so far, then again.

'Did he even like chocolates?' Garry asked. 'I never saw him eating them.'

Garry had a point. Strange as it was, not everybody enjoyed that kind of confectionery.

'It's quite expensive, I think.' Julia said thoughtfully. 'I expected if he didn't like chocolates, someone would have popped out and got him a tube of Pringles.'

Gary nodded in agreement. 'It was expensive. I don't suppose they'd worry about a thing like that. Only...' Gary's eyes narrowed. 'It was odd. One minute, Tanner had nothing. The next, he'd got himself every penny of his target and five pounds sixty more. The sandwich and crisps were on a meal deal. So five sixty would have been enough.' The perplexed PC looked Julia in the eye. 'Who would have thought it, eh? That all that money would come flooding in last minute, just before it was announced that he'd killed Her Ladyship.'

Who would have thought, indeed?

16

NIGHT WATCH

It felt odd, being back in her cottage. Julia couldn't help but think that maybe she'd forgotten something. She left a little piece of the person that Julia was before the incarceration behind in that cold concrete cell with its hard cot and its high window. She stopped sleeping, finding herself wandering around the house in the early hours, munching through an entire loaf of toasted white bread and trying to work out what it was exactly that had happened and why she was suffering from such chronic indigestion.

'You've had yourself a shock,' Carris said sympathetically as they sat in front of Julia's hearth, with golden flames flickering brightly in front of them and mugs of hot tea in hand. 'You're bound to feel a little out of sorts.'

Julia smiled sadly. She had taken a week off from her duties. It was needed in order to get the matter straight in her head. Something wouldn't stop worrying her. Only now, what with the constant indigestion, the midnight wandering, and the forever busy toaster, Julia felt a sneaking sense of guilt—guilt that Julia couldn't seem to brush aside since the last means of communication which Her Ladyship had received on this bright, beautiful earth had been an irritated letter from an irate library manager. A letter which implied, although it didn't state, that Her Ladyship was, in fact, a waste of space and the planet would be a whole heap better without her. Harsh, by anybody's reckoning.

In writing that letter and posting it through Her Ladyship's door, Julia had gone against one of her very own tenets, the things she felt supported the very fabric of her life: never say, write or do anything that you wouldn't want emblazoned on the front page of a newspaper or worn by everybody you know in the form of a T-shirt. Julia might be innocent of the murder, but she had unwittingly and selfishly given the woman a push into isolation, and none of that was nice.

However, leaving *nice* to one side, this was still a murder case. After his letter of confusion, Mark Tanner had sent a postcard from Dignitas. It was a simple two-word inscription. Mark's postcard said simply: "By all." He had misspelt his last salute to the world—a sad but true fact. Mark had not even been a product of the local school. Luckily, almost everyone else who read it had been. So, the spelling mistake went unnoticed. Regi at the Dog and Duck had framed the thing and stuck it on the wall above the bar in Mark's favourite spot. This gesture had seemed, to Julia, somehow too jovial. It didn't reflect the true gravitas of the situation, and therefore, it was out of place. In displaying the card above the bar, it seemed as if the deaths, both Mark's and Her Ladyship's, had been jokes, like the sort of story you recount with a laugh after a few pints of beer—or cider (if your inclination was more apples than hops).

Sitting in her front room with the fire roaring in front of her, Julia took a long, hard sip of her tea. 'Something about this, Carris, it just doesn't stack up,' she pulled her cheeks together in thought as if literally chewing over the problem.

'The picture on Mark's postcard was very boring.' Julia conceded thoughtfully. 'Dignitas isn't big on stationery. Embarrassing, really.' Her features brightened. 'The library could teach them a thing or two on that front. Do you think I should contact them?' Luckily, the question was more rhetorical, demanding no answer. 'Although,' Carris paused, clearly hitting a complication. 'I can't imagine they'd be needing the tote bags.'

'Everyone needs a tote bag,' Julia said, which was, of course, a fundamental axiom of human existence.

'Oh, Julia.' Carris exclaimed. 'How on earth could they have suspected you?!' The young library assistant shot her exasperated eyes towards the heavens at the sheer effrontery of such a thing.

'Well, there were the letters,' Julia shifted awkwardly in her chair

Carris waved a dismissive hand. 'That was just a gentle reminder.'

Julia shook her head. 'I threatened legal action and public humiliation.'

'Hmm,' Carris looked thoughtful. 'The legal action, well...' she shrugged, 'in this village, that's hardly surprising. But...' She tilted her head to one side. 'I can't help being curious about the public humiliation. What exactly did you have in mind?'

Julia sighed. 'I hadn't really thought it through. I simply went in all guns blazing without a plan.'

Carris pursed her lips. 'Not like you.'

'Not at all.'

Carris placed her china cup back on the coffee table, having mused through the idea of public humiliation. 'I mean, there is always the stocks. The ones they stick the teachers in, so they can throw wet sponges at them on fete days, general fundraisers and Shrove Tuesday.'

'True,' Julia said. 'Although without the use of the common, that would have proved tricky.'

'Impossible,' Carris conceded. 'You know, Julia. I did rather like the shots of you in the tree,' Carris said sweetly. 'I asked PC Mumblings if he could run me off a copy so I could get one framed, but he was being a jobsworth about it.'

Julia nodded. She didn't bother to tell Carris that she had asked Gary to destroy the images. They were hardly flattering, and besides, Julia didn't want any reminders of her antics up at the Hall.

'Anyway,' Carris said brightly, sliding her thin buttocks back into the comfortable armchair which Julia always gave up for her guests. 'It's all done now.'

For a moment, there was silence. A silence so deep you could hear the clock in the next-door cottage ticking through the partition wall.

'The problem is,' Julia said slowly. 'I can't see that Mark was the murdering type.'

'He confessed.' Carris said quickly.

'But Mark? He was ancient.'

'Exactly.' Carris said lightly, brushing a few crumbs from her tan A-line skirt. The one she always wore for visiting. 'Old enough to know exactly what he was doing.' And at that, she fixed Julia with an oddly firm gaze. 'You never can tell, Julia. Mark Tanner did have some odd interests.'

'But naturism and murder? I'm not sure that the two are natural bed partners.'

Carris looked shocked.

'Just an expression; perhaps I should have said natural fit.' Julia waved an arm dismissively, bored with semantics. She had found, since her incarceration, that she was falling prone to odd thoughts. Ever since her brush with the law, Julia's mind seemed to flit in all directions, as though she knew there was a mystery here somewhere, one that needed to be unravelled but couldn't quite find the end of it and therefore had no idea what threads she should be pulling on. Julia knew that paranoia was a big label with an entire medical discipline stacked up behind it. It was certainly not a term to be bandied about lightly unless, of course, you were Alfred Hitchcock, which seemed highly unlikely since the poor man was quite clearly dead. Paranoia, in its boiled-down form, denoted an exaggeration of circumstance—a tendency to tie random events into intricate patterns of cause and effect—random patterns in which one places oneself at the centre. Julia did not want to feel at the centre of what was going on here, in this small rural village, but despite the denials, despite Mark's cheery postcard announcing his departure and despite the warm welcome she had received on her return from the cold concrete cell; the library manager was all too aware that something was badly amiss—something big.

Julia had been on the receiving end of the devastating consequences of a miscarriage of justice. This was not paranoia; this was fact, and she did not want to get roped in again, yet something about the Tanner confession troubled her. She took her tea to the window, parting the pretty net curtains, which she washed twice a year, the ones that smelt of laundry powder and flower meadows, parting them so she could see into the street outside.

'I just feel...' Julia said, letting her voice trail away.

'Oh?' Carris asked, hanging off the librarian's every word.

And yet sadly, and totally uncharacteristically, Julia could not put her finger on exactly what it was that she did feel.

~

SINCE ARRIVING IN THE VILLAGE, Julia had always lived on the council estate at the end of town. It had been built at a time when the rural planners understood that a person, a family, or a human being would need more than a regulation cat-swinging space in order to be happy. Nobody in their right mind wanted to swing a cat. Even if they had read *Not Giving a Furball* or *Zen and the Art of Cat Apathy* and were, therefore, in full comprehension as to the true nature of their (not so committed) feline "friends." However, many people liked to indulge in windmilling their arms (no cat attached). It was good for upper body toning as well as enhancing a spirit of freedom and attracting Chi—life force.

The council houses in the village were generous and in a wonderful location. Not on the large green in the old part of the town, but standing proud and a little raised on the road out. They stood at an elevated position, ensuring wonderful views of the entire area. Most of the houses had been snapped up when Margaret Thatcher decided to sell the entire country off bit by bit, brick by brick, utility by utility. Therefore, a degree of individualism had crept into the pebble-dash estate. Porches, doors and curtains were a perennial favourite for self-expression. Julia had satisfied herself with white lace curtains. For others, Venetian blinds had been popular in the eighties, but they proved difficult to maintain and easy to break, and they were irritating for those who had children as the swinging chord proved to be a permanent temptation. Most people replaced the Venetians with the canvas pull-down types, which often contained colourful pictures or, on occasion, the continental wooden shutters, which looked so very contemporary but cost a small fortune. Terry from Turbo Tinkers had decided to make do with newspaper. There were no planning restrictions, so the attitude regarding window dressing was, in a sense, laissez-faire. For people coming from out of town, Terry's newspaper improvisation might have seemed odd, sinister even. However, everybody in the estate knew Terry had very greasy fingers on account of all the cars he was trying to keep roadworthy. So, a fresh sheet of newspaper always did the trick when winter closed in.

The estate of pebble-dash houses curved around a small strip of playing field with its own basketball hoop and a number of swings. On a summer's evening, you could hear the kiddies playing catch out on the field till late at night, and every Thursday, come rain or shine, Captain Crispy's fish and chip van would draw up in the layby and start to fry. For many, it was the highlight of the week. The local supermarket did have a café, but there was nothing so delicious as a rectangle of potato fried fast and furious, crusted with salt and laced with vinegar. Most of the estate would meet over a cone of chips for a chat. Only this Thursday, Julia had not gone. No. She had not wanted to chat. It seemed to Julia as if all she had been getting since her release were sympathetic looks and pity. Nobody liked pity. Before her stay at the station, the woman had been a pillar of the community. A person that people sought out for her wisdom, advice and wit. Since the arrest, all of that had changed. People were only interested in handing her hankies or telling her they understood, which they so clearly didn't. And so Julia stood behind the safety of her windows, her lace curtains parted, watching.

Since it was October, the street was already dark by the time the van arrived. Normally, a few stragglers would go out to greet it, but most of the estate would hang back, especially in the cool of winter. They'd wait for the fat to get hot and the potato to start sizzling. Only that night, the Thursday after Julia got out of jail, things seemed to be operating differently. As soon as the van arrived, everyone poured out of their houses. The frying trailer was mobbed. Julia wondered briefly if the Captain (this was his actual title - the chip van was merely a sideline – since, during the summer months, he worked on a cruising vessel which set sail out of Kings Lynn in Norfolk) had come from another town and was selling the crispy bits from the bottom of the fryer, which was always a treat, for a knockdown price. But no, this couldn't be right because some people didn't even wait for the oil to heat before the Captain handed them a small package wrapped tightly in a sheet of newspaper.

Julia squinted into the night, wishing she had a pair of binoculars. What on earth could be going on out there? What on earth was it that those scurrying back towards their houses were clutching in their hands? Could it be pickled eggs? No, that was ludicrous. Not everyone liked a pickled egg. Therefore, not everyone would be scurrying away with them. Pickled eggs were an acquired taste. If you hadn't tasted their delights before the age of eight, you would, most likely, never be converted. And yet, whatever they were carrying, every single person seemed furtive, yet strangely delighted. Something was going on. Sadly, Julia could not for the life of her think what it could be.

Taking herself up to her bedroom, she looked down on the village. Sure enough, it was a hive of activity. People passed each other quickly in the street, holding something small and neat. It was barely bigger than a palm. It couldn't be eggs. It simply couldn't be.

Julia waited till the village had fallen asleep. It was around two thirty in the morning when the last light went out, and the village fell into a deep sleep. As quiet as a mouse, Julia took her coat down from its hook, grabbed her flashlight from the useful drawer, and took her keys from the bowl before walking out into the tonight. She walked three whole laps around the village looking for something, anything, which seemed out of place. But the village was sleeping. The streets, the roads, and the gardens were all holding onto their secret. Paranoia. Julia thought to herself, as she arrived back at her estate, walking quickly past the basketball hoop. It must have been pickled eggs. If she had just gone out to get herself a cone of chips from the van, the mystery would have been solved. If she had just acted normally, she'd be tucked up in bed by now, safe and asleep. Her head would be resting on her lavender pillow. Taking her keys back out of her bag, she chided herself for her foolishness. And as the light fell from the fob, which she always kept on her key chain, her heart skipped a beat. For there on the floor, outside Terry's, was a scrap of newspaper. This, in itself would not have been unusual. After all, the man used paper instead of curtains. Perhaps he had simply been installing a fresh new look. Yet as Julia looked back towards Terry's house, she realised not one window was covered up. There must have been a paper shortage in the village that night. One which Terry had been happy to fix. She bent towards the sheet which lay abandoned on the ground. Odder still, this paper was not ironed flat for the purpose of covering windows but crinkled. It was crinkled and creased as though it had been wrapped around something tightly, something precious and something that somebody had not wanted to be seen. Bending a little further, Julia gently picked up the paper, and to her consternation, wrapped inside the broadsheet, she discovered one small straggly, sorry for itself, bit of a plant.

17

AND SO IT GOES

As it turned out, nobody was surprised when Julia said she wanted to pull an early retirement. The woman had been through a lot, and as always, the community was in full support. Carris had done remarkably well during Julia's incarceration. The library alarm system had only been triggered seventeen times in total, which wasn't bad at all, considering Julia had been gone for seventy-two hours and forty-five minutes. What was surprising was that the ex-library manager wished her retirement to take effect immediately.

Julia didn't want to go back to work. The reason for this appeared to be two-fold: she was keen for the freedom that retirement would undoubtedly allow, but perhaps even more importantly, she had noticed a growing attraction blossoming between Carris and young Des—the postman. Some people actually said that Des and Carris had been setting the alarm off just for fun. Whatever the truth of this particular story, it was apparent that Des had been borrowing Carris' Bongo on his afternoons off and that Carris had been seen wearing Des' peaked postman's hat at a jaunty angle and accessorised with a string of laughter. So, there was that. If more explanation was needed—Julia wanted time to work on her leaving speech. She didn't wish to be outdone by the Reverend Tibbs, who she personally found a little preachy. As luck would have it, Carris had already put the bare-bones of the leaving do in place. So, hitting the delivery button on the event did not present a problem.

And therefore, twenty years after the concerns over the leylandii hedge, Almost two years after Lord Hortishall had sadly passed away, three months after the final Hortishall bombshell about the common, and only two weeks after Lady Hortishall had been found dead in the conservatory on her Persian rug, this was the time in which the community gathered in the room above the pub to bid farewell to their beloved Julia.

They clapped when the ex-library manager entered, wearing a fresh navy outfit which had been donated by Ruth Silverling. It looked a treat despite the fact that it had Ruth's logo sneakily sewn across the back. Julia was aware of the logo but did not mind, knowing well enough that there was no such thing as a free lunch.

For a woman over sixty, it had to be admitted that the ex-library manager appeared to be glowing. The terror of her stint in jail had left no visible scars. She was barely through the door before little Bethany tottered towards her, the child's arms loaded with lilies. Her mother, Gemma, ushered the girl forward, checking that Bethany's hands were fully occupied. Nobody wanted a repeat performance of Bethany's nasal passages in action. The re-appropriation of the maypole ribbon had not been forgotten. For a moment, Julia found herself turning away—hit by a shaft of emotion. The celebration seemed glorious and heart-breaking all rolled into one.

'Bethany,' Julia took the flowers gratefully from the child, the sweet scent rising from their lush, open petals. 'And Gemma!' A tear formed in Julia's eye, and a lump of emotion rose in her throat. 'Look at me,' she laughed. 'I've come over all emotional.' She gave one final sniff before placing the flowers on the table behind her and continued on with her speech. 'For over thirty years,' she said, 'I have been library manager.' A little cheer rippled through the audience. Many lifted their glasses of cider in a silent toast. 'They said it would be difficult,' Julia said with a smile, 'to enter such a tight-knit community.' She glanced around her at the people she had come to think of as her friends. A wall of smiling, familiar faces and genuine warmth looked back at her. 'I can honestly say,' she clutched her chest, 'I do feel as if I belong. 'Little Gemma.' Julia turned her attention back to the newly minted lawyer. 'The first time I came across you, you were just a tiddler, and now you've finished your final year at law school!'

A round of heart-felt clapping circulated the room.

'Not that I'm surprised.' Julia reached out and touched the younger woman's arm affectionately. 'Gemma has always had the determination of a pit bull terrier.'

Gemma blushed, truly flattered.

'Young Gemma read *Ulysses*, aged only fifteen, without incurring one late fine.'

There was a brief cheer from the gathered. Even though most of them would not have known what or who *Ulysses* was. The local school, Saint Martin's in the Meadow, left much to be desired. Despite this, Julia had always found that most of the villages were brought up well, knowing, at a bare minimum, when a smile or nod was most likely needed, even when understanding didn't happen to be available. Although, she would have to admit that they were all totally clueless when faced with the cutlery of a four-course meal. But as Regi Brewhound, the landlord of the establishment in which they were now gathered, maintained, there was no need to stand on ceremony with sustenance since human beings came out of the box with fingers attached. Besides, these things can all be learned if you find yourself a copy of the right book.

'And my dear colleague and friend...' Julia turned her watering eyes towards Carris. 'I shall be sorry to let you go, but people...' she turned back to the congregation. 'You are in safe hands. As I always say,' Julia eyed the room, drinking them all in. 'Forget Shakespeare. It is books, not eyes, that are the windows to the soul. The council cuts to the library system...'

Mr Perkins had not been invited.

'Well, short-sighted, that's what that is. People need communal spaces. Besides...' She allowed herself a brief, barely audible tut. 'A good librarian is worth her weight in gold. I could have saved the NHS a great deal of money by giving an early diagnosis of Mrs Talbot's Munchausen with *Maladies you never knew existed* combined with extended borrowing of *Twenty Ways to Keep Your Doctor On His Toes*.

'A self-service machine can't do that.' Des shouted from the audience, not even bothering to apologise for interrupting.

How things had changed—meek Des, always so fast with the apologies, there he was interrupting for all he was worth. Julia noticed that Carris clutched one hand over her chest in awe at the man's astuteness within the context of this keynote presentation.

'Exactly, Des. Thank you.' Julia said, for it was important

to give encouragement where encouragement might be helpful. 'And it's not just books that speak volumes,' she said with a sense of stoicism—one that can only be achieved through studying philosophy or working within the library system. 'Reading habits provoke conversation. People like to explain why they're borrowing certain books. They might say, "Charley Dickens—I'm studying him at night school" or "Keeping Goats—I'm thinking of going into the cheese-making business."'

'That was me,' Angie said, laughing, raising another glass of cider to her lips.

'And very good your cheese was too, Angie.' Julia rejoiced; credit where credit was due. What could be more perfect on a summer's evening than a glass of local cider, a slice of apple and a crumbly bit of goat's cheese? Julia felt emotion welling up inside her at all the things she would be saying goodbye to when, at the end of this glorious reception, with its coloured bunting, finger food and proliferation of cheesy Wotsits, she would walk from the large swinging doors of the pub and mount her bike for the last time.

'ALL IN ALL,' she continued, 'over the years, I've gotten to know more about my fellow villagers than is perhaps strictly necessary.' There were a couple of engaged nods in the room. However, feeling herself on a roll, Julia did not stop for interjection, holding up one arm to quell a low rustle of chatter. 'But to be perfectly candid, these past few months, and then this murder, well, it has, so to speak, put the cat amongst the pigeons.'

The grumbles grew, and once again, Julia raised her hand. 'It may appear to many of you that I had not been as involved as some in the proceedings—reference the common.' She took a deep breath. 'So, it's only fair now, I feel, at this point in time...' She felt her mouth beginning to dry and reached instinctively for the glass of water Carris had set on the table next to her, ready and waiting. 'Well,' she said, returning the water to the table, having satisfied her thirst. 'It might be best to lay my cards on the table. As some of you may or may not be aware, I had always admired the library at Hortishall Hall.'

She could see Reece sinking down in his chair, wanting to avoid attention.

'Although not officially open to the public, I had found the Royal British Legion Fete on the first Sunday in June to be fortuitous. It was perfectly plausible to lose one's way in search of the lavatories.'

There were a few bursts of laughter—Beatrice Bell, for one. Clearly, it wasn't just Julia who had taken the opportune moment of the open garden to take a gander around the house.

'It was well worth a visit,' Julia continued, half wondering what Beatrice's specialist interest at the Hall had been—no doubt something connected with organs. But that was Beatrice's story, not Julia's. And this was not Beatrice's day, as indicated by the invitation which had been circulated —"no mechanical devices to be brought onto the premises." Julia gave a brief shake of her head, knowing that she needed to return to the job at hand, having important information to impart.

'The Hortishall library,' Julia said, a little more decisively, 'had a number of first editions, some signed.' She smiled. 'There was even an Eliot with a lovely dedication and a doodle of a butterfly. I'm not sure if Eliot actually did the doodle or someone added that at a later date.' She brushed an imaginary bit of fluff from the shoulders of her blue dress. She knew her speech would get harder from here on in as she tried to ease herself into it gently. 'I can't say as I wasn't disappointed never to have received an official invitation. However, I found comfort in the will—Lord Hortishall's Last Will and Testament. You see, I heard things from our...' She cleared her throat, 'local solicitor Reece Trumpington. Please put your hand up, Reece, so everyone can see where you are.'

An awkward hand was reluctantly raised. Understandably, Reece was looking shifty and sheepish at the back of the room, talking to no one.

'That's right.' Julia said. 'Don't be shy. Now...' she continued, now the man's whereabouts were established for all. 'Reece reads books which I would class as porn.'

Gemma slipped her hands over Bethany's ears as a nervous titter of laughter rotated around the room.

'Reece, on the other hand,' Julia continued, 'would class them as having a mildly erotic nature. Isn't that right, Reece?'

The man said nothing; he just took a moment to examine his shoes.

That was fine. Julia didn't need a reply. 'And that, of course, is why Reece is always so keen to talk when returning his library books, and, I would add, the reason for him pressuring head office for a self-service machine.'

It was noted that the poor solicitor was turning a little red.

'Reece opens the book,' Julia continued, 'offering me the barcode like he's trying to be helpful. But I don't need to see the jackets of "Babes of Babylon" or "Three Large Ladies on a Camel" to know that these are not biblical texts.'

There was a snort of schoolboy laughter. It was uncertain where the guttural grunt originated from, and most likely, it wasn't relevant.

'It was many years ago, whilst Reece was deploying his diversion tactics, that I first heard a faint whiff of Lord Hortishall's proposed gift. The information was a bit mumbled. I had a full library that day and a lot on. So, one Christmas, I took our local solicitor to this very pub and made sure his sherry glass was full and that his hands were never short of a mince pie. The information I gathered was worth it.' She narrowed her eyes and scanned the room, not wanting those assembled to miss the import of what she was about to say. 'A quarter of all the books at the Hall had been bequeathed to our small library. And that is why when Lord Hortishall passed over, the emotion that I felt was not exactly one of having endured a great loss. I had only met him twice. On the first occasion, he said, "Third door on the left," and on the second, "Mind the hot tap; these old houses have unpredictable plumbing." He was always very polite, but it's not as if we had regular communication. So, when he departed, I waited with a sense of eager anticipation to be summoned to the great house. I was so excited about the prospect of this magnanimous gift that I could barely sleep. I took to staring out of my cottage windows most nights, eager for time to move on. And this, I might add, is a foolish thing to do when you are heading towards sixty. But, these books would have ensured library funds for many years to come. They were valuable items. Don't get me wrong, I was worried about the common.'

A chorus of angry 'hear, hears!' bubbled up.

'But it was the bequeathment of the books that I had to protect.' Julia continued, 'And soon, I was simply too busy to enter much into the debate regarding the common itself since an anonymous donation of thousands of books had appeared on the library steps,' she wrinkled her nose at the memory. 'Cheap paperbacks, damp and dusty. I couldn't work out what was happening. It was only after I looked inside the second box that it dawned on me who might have donated such a "gift."' Julia's normally open and welcoming eyes narrowed into hard points of flint. 'What was disappointing, Reece,' she said, looking directly at the man, 'was that someone I considered a friend was involved in the pulp fiction Hortishall hoax.'

This was all too much. Reece got to his feet. It was clear that the man was a shadow of his former self. His shoulders stooped, and his face was pale and as clammy as warm wax. Despite what he had done, the drastic shock of his appearance caused people's hearts to soften. 'I'm so sorry,' he said. 'What I did was nothing less than dastardly. I colluded with Her Ladyship.' He shrugged. 'She offered me fifty per cent of all profits from the book sale. At the time, I happened to be financially compromised.'

'A woman,' Silas shouted angrily. Truth be told, Silas was a misogynist. There were those in the village who had actually relished the idea of the man being marooned safely, without exit or entry points, in his cottage on the green.

'No,' Reece shook his head. 'Without going into detail, it was an experiment in quantum dynamics.'

The room nodded. Reece was right; no detail was needed, and besides, it was best not to go down this avenue as it sounded very much like it could lure them all unwittingly into trouble and unfounded allegations of an extraterrestrial nature, yet again.

Reece ran one spindly hand through his steel grey hair before puffing out his chest in an attempt to stand tall. 'I have since sold the books and donated the proceeds to the library.'

People nodded in agreement. The overall attitude was maybe the man wasn't such a bad egg after all. Although, even linking Reece in the imagination with eggs, and therefore raptors and lizards, was most definitely a bad idea.

'I ask for forgiveness.' Reece said, with a touching and very human air of humility. 'I got a bit above myself.'

'Aw,' a few people said sympathetically. After all, getting above oneself was indeed unfortunate but easy enough to do, especially when one had sky-high aspirations. It looked for once as though Reece had finally come back down to earth. 'She was a loathsome woman,' the local solicitor said. 'And I am sorry for the distress I have caused.' He took his seat once again, and a number of people patted him on the back sympathetically, much like you might pat a dog, a cat or a creature which was not entirely humanoid but posed no threat. In truth, there had been no love lost over Lady Hortishall. Her funeral service might have been packed, but it was clear that everyone present had gone for all the wrong reasons, and the subsequent party after the event went on for days, almost drinking the pub dry and getting through one year's harvest from Angie's barn.

'I have always maintained,' Julia said, returning to the thought of Her Ladyship. 'That it is unwise to make enemies in a small rural community.'

There were more than a number of nods in the wake of this sentence.

'They found Lady Hortishall,' Julia continued, 'sitting in the conservatory as neat and bloodless as a clean pin. The only things broken were one painted bone china tea cup and a wafer-thin almond biscuit.'

Gareth from the Gazette rapped his fingers in a trill of agreement on his notebook, which was laid open for comment. He had printed all the details as soon as he'd been given access. It was not every day that someone in the village died—someone who was so unpopular that a number of jaunty ditties had been written in the woman's dishonour. Unfortunately, the songs could not be sung at Julia's retirement event due to their colourful nature and the presence of young children. However, a number of choir members had said that you couldn't really call Bethany a child since she was prone to shocking outbursts of physical ability and was constantly subjecting the community to unwanted, unasked-for demonstrations of the wonders of her nasal passage. According to the girl's passport, however, Bethany was still a minor, and therefore protection was needed.

'Now, murder,' Julia said, running her eyes over the audience, making sure she was holding them all with her words, 'as you know, is big business in the book industry. Our crime section inhabits three carousels. Not to mention Large Crime—large print, that is, not large as in high body count. But, of course, there are different types of murder. Most people don't want graphic detail. They want a nice, tidy, comfortable murder, clean and aesthetic in a rural setting, with lots of motive, which is exactly what we had. In order to compose my speech,' Julia cleared her throat. 'I have sought help from another council employee, PC Mumblings.' Julia held out a hand to credit the man. He was not wearing his uniform as he usually did on social occasions. Instead, he was dressed in a beetle-green polo and a pair of tan chinos with pleats so pressed you could cut butter with them. He looked almost normal sat as he was next to Marsha. She had given up her job at Reece's. It had all been too much for her. Besides, she had sights on a brighter future. Marsha had proposed to PC Mumblings that they set up their own detective agency. It was unclear whether this would happen or, indeed, if such an endeavour were a good idea. However, nobody liked a doom-monger, so Julia was keeping shtum. Besides, Gary had been very helpful to the ex-library manager, who had missed so many of the proceedings. Helpful enough, in fact, to go blow-by-blow through the workings of the Hortishall case.

'I have it on good authority,' Julia said as Gary gave a quick glance around the room, hoping that nobody from the constabulary had crept in. Tactfully, the villagers did not return his gaze, and Julia continued. 'Whilst I was still under his majesty's protection, the village turned to Gwyn Thomas. Gwyn has read every Agatha Christie ever written.' Julia angled her attention to the grey-haired lady sitting at the front of the room with her book bag at her heels. 'Isn't that right, Gwyn?'

Gwyn nodded, feeling more than a little awkward, not quite sure where this was going or happy about having herself highlighted. But Julia had no intention of stopping. 'Gwyn's aptitude for understanding the criminal mind is truly a marvel. Word got around,' Julia said, eyeing the room, 'as word does, that the cause of death was poison—the almond biscuit. If you remember, Her Ladyship was found with such a delicacy crumpled on the floor. Arsenic tastes of almonds. Gwyn, no doubt, deduced from the biscuit that the crime had been committed by a woman. Women go for crimes involving baking. Men are far more inclined to strangulation, shooting, or electrocution. Mind you,' Julia held up one hand to quell a persistent murmur which was kicking off and gave a nod towards Gemma—knowing that she could easily find herself on tricky ground here. 'You can't just go saying things like that. Not in today's climate. You have to be politically correct, or offence will be taken. Sure enough, Pierre, the chef at *le Maison de Chien*, took umbrage. Isn't that right, Pierre?'

'*Bien sûr*,' Pierre replied with his lovely French accent. Not genuine, of course, but still quite a beauty. It was acquired through repeated, and possibly obsessive, viewings of classical French cinema from the 1950s to 1960s. He was, as was so often the case with a chef, a little on the obsessive side. Even now, he was still in his chef's whites, with his tall paper hat, despite the fact that it was actually his day off. Pierre was a man who had been told as a child by a French actress who played a bit part in a Truffaut film that he looked good in a hat, so for that very reason, he rarely took it off.

'You argued, Pierre,' Julia said, 'that you could, in fact, make a more appetising almond biscuit out of a bit of arsenic than the entire membership of the Young Wives Association.'

At this audacity, there was an audible gasp. A number of the Young Wives, led by the lovely Marta Harris, stood to make their exit.

'Please,' Pierre said, his tone full of apology. 'I have very cold hands,' he explained. 'Their constant low temperature makes my pastry unavoidably outstanding in its quality.' He glanced over to the group of petticoated, pretty women. 'It is, therefore, not a level playing field. I have an advantage.' He dropped his eyes guiltily, gazing towards those wonderful hands. 'It is an advantage not on account of gender but because of my Raynaud's.'

'An unfortunate condition,' offered Dr Flo Carter, 'causing extreme coldness in the fingertips.'

Pierre shrugged. 'It is my super power.'

'Exactly,' Julia said, remembering how Pierre had

ordered *Embrace the Chill: Raynauld's Secret to Baking Brilliance* from the inter-library loan system only last year.

She cleared her throat, taking a moment to garner herself. 'I don't have to tell you all that the women of the village found Pierre's comments difficult to digest.'

'I'm sorry,' Olivia Dentlow, the hygienist, said, having married two months previously to a lovely young woman possessing an entirely different kitbag of apparatus than the much-despised Ben Wiseman (he of the coffee-dental-sabotage scheme.) Olivia knew how damaging tittle-tattle could be. She hadn't meant to join in with the rumours or implicate Pierre in the murder. 'I hadn't realised how seductive gossip is,' she said sadly, fluttering her long, pretty lashes, and was, of course, therefore, immediately forgiven.

'Please,' Pierre, said magnanimously. 'This is nothing. A storm in a teacup.'

'Exactly,' Julia snapped into action. 'When I was incarcerated myself, the police hauled Pierre in for questioning. However, as it turned out, the biscuit was a bit of a red herring. It was the tea. The tea contained the poison.'

Sal dropped her eyes awkwardly to the floor. She was known to serve three types of tea at the Snippy Biscuit, two of which Sal was unsure as to how she should even pronounce their names. Like so many, Sal secretly yearned for simpler times—times when the multifaceted hot beverage was mostly just referred to as Builder's Brew.

'At first,' Julia continued, 'the police thought the poison was deadly nightshade, a crop which grows abundantly outside the headquarters of the Halesworth Harmony Hut. And every single last member of the choir was hauled down to the station and made to sing, so to speak, about their botanical knowledge. The caretaker, none other than Clive Corpusty, a man who, as we all know, is not keen on boy's activities and was reluctant to provide an overnight stay for the poor, frozen Mia Chung.'

'All perfectly reasonable,' Clive said quickly in his defence. 'My hut is a place for recreational activity, and Mia was clearly done with every conceivable kind of recreational involvement.'

'It might be best to drop the "my", Reverend Tibbs offered. 'The hut is community property. Besides, it is easier for a camel...'

'There were no camels involved,' Clive said quickly, shooting an irritated toward of Reece—a man who had such unfortunate borrowing habits, ones that clearly involved dromedaries. 'It was only a unicycle and a chainsaw,' Clive continued, 'and Curtis took the heavy machinery back with him as soon as it had thawed out.'

Julia realised that the conversation was descending into anarchy and rapped her knuckles sharply in a call for quiet against the improvised podium.

'I'm talking police procedural here...' she said loudly, and the room fell into welcomed silence. 'Good, so, as I was saying, Clive Corpusty—him with the twinkle in his eye, was a prime candidate.'

'I find that...' Clive started.

'Clive, we all know about your foraging and your love of poisonous plants. Some of which are pretty.'

PC Mumblings nodded. 'That's what they said at the station. Especially the fox gloves.'

Julia shook her head in dismay and shot PC Gary Mumblings an ironic look. 'But Gary, if the police had only thought to ask me, I could have told them not to bother with Clive. Two years ago, he ordered *Plants to Help You Stay Younger*, which clearly explains how belladonna makes the pupils dilate.'

'I only wanted to knock a decade or so off,' Clive said sheepishly. 'I'm so envious of the activities available to young men these days. I wanted to get that Peter Pan effect.'

'Don't we all?' Julia said curtly. 'Luckily,' Julia continued. 'The pathologist managed to save poor Clive's neck though not his pride.' She turned her attention to the sheepish caretaker. 'Don't be bashful, Clive. It's all in the past. The poison which killed Her Ladyship was a form of Datura, of which deadly nightshade is one, but it had a different genetic makeup.'

'Silas,' Julia called out, making the poor marooned Silas feel even more at sea. 'You came under scrutiny for your tomatoes. Megan Keeble, your aubergines were up for examination.' Megan shrank into her shoulders. 'All are forms of Datura, but the toxins in these plants are negligible. You'd have to eat a mountain of hairy vines before you felt even the tiniest bit queasy. The entire quiz team was quizzed as to their knowledge of other people's horticultural preferences. People were encouraged to inform. The police were looking for a perennial with large trumpet-shaped flowers. With it being early October, the earth remained obstinately quiet, giving the murderer,' she paused for effect here, 'more than enough time to dispose of the root.

When the letter was delivered from Mark Tanner - the one apologising for murdering Her Ladyship but explaining that he wanted to do one last thing of significance before he headed off to Switzerland to meet his maker - there had been no flowers out. Not at that time of year. The Datura had disappeared. There was not one clue. I myself went into the library. It was a day well spent. I withdrew from circulation the book which our lovely artist Artie had checked in shortly before the murder *Handy Plants for Awkward Corners*.

Julia glanced towards Artie, who was suddenly looking

very hot under the collar. He shifted in his seat, about to stand. 'Artie, sit. I'm not done yet.'

Julia picked up her handbag from the floor and took out a small, crumpled shopping list.

'As you can see, the book in question still holds Artie's book marker—a shopping list which indicates, Artie, that you are not long for this world yourself: a packet of Marlboro, some frozen chips, a white sliced loaf, a litre bottle of whisky, and a "monster" size bag of Doritos.'

Artie looked awkward. But everyone knew about his Dorito habit. What was uncertain was if he was drinking the whisky to hide the smell of the highly flavoured crisps or eating the crisps to mask the smell of the booze. Either way, Julia was right. Artie needed to put himself on a bit of a boot camp. However, currently, that was not her primary concern.

'If you had time to bypass Artie's shopping list,' she said, placing the item to one side, '...and examine the pages of the actual book, you would note the description of a rather interesting Datura, one which is described as having attractive trumpet-shaped flowers but an unfortunate toxic habit. Artie had the motive—Her Ladyship had made him feel like a fool. She tricked him into talking about hay bales—a situation which had prompted the annexing of the common.'

'But I...' The poor lad looked panic-stricken. It was not, after all, every day that one got accused of murder as well as having poor nutritional inclinations.

'However,' Julia said, 'It could be argued that every person here has a motive.' The gathered withered under her gaze. She cleared her throat. 'I have noticed the people in this particular community do like to help each other out. Although, it has not slipped my attention that plant cuttings are being circulated.' She shot the Captain a hard look;

using a chip van for criminal activity was always a little underhand. 'No doubt', Julia continued, feeling a little confidence swell through her body, proud to have rumbled such a water-tight conspiracy. 'No doubt next year there will be a proliferation of trumpet-shaped Daturas. After all, if Mark Tanner's confession were ever to be discredited, it would simply not be possible to prosecute an entire town.' She dipped another hand into her bag, this time pulling out Mark's hastily written postcard, which was not, in fact, misspelt. 'By All.' She said simply. Leaving the room to sweat for just one moment before ripping Mark's confession of cunning community cohesion in half. 'It doesn't take many to inflate a CashSplash page, and it's abundantly clear from the charity website that you all did your bit.'

A murmur of fear passed around the room, but Julia held up one large, calming hand. 'Rest assured, friends, as library manager, I have signed the Data Protection Act. Good heavens,' she laughed, raising her eyes to the ceiling. 'No one would take any books out if they thought we'd go blabbing their reading habits all over the county. So, I shall take the information with me to the grave via Florida. Mr Eliot...' Again, Julia reached into her bag, taking a small book gently from the silk lining of her purse and holding it aloft for all to see. 'This should more than pay for a modest lifestyle on the West Coast.' She smiled, and her face truly did light up in joy. 'A butterfly inside,' she said, as though marvelling at the very idea. 'Who would have thought the great man was prone to doodling? Which just goes to prove,' She smiled sweetly at all those gathered before her. 'You never should judge a book by its cover.'

A NOTE FROM THE PUBLISHER

Thank you for reading this book. If you enjoyed it please do consider leaving a review on Amazon.

We hate typos. If you find any, let the team know and we can get it amended. publishedwithpassion@aol.com

PUBLISHED WITH PASSION

ALSO AVAILABLE

Person of Interest

A moneymaking opportunity turns into a murder mystery for a young real estate agent.

Real estate is a competitive business. Kirstin likes to work the angles—she keeps an eye on the obituaries and has a mortician notify her when a property's about to go on the market. The latest tip could lead to a big payoff: a famed child psychologist has died, and the stunning Milford estate on an idyllic Cornish island is about to become available.

Kirstin makes sure to mingle with the bereaved and pass along her business card. However, when she witnesses an apparent blackmail attempt and a near-fatal accident, Kirstin decides it's time to leave. But with the local roads closed, she can't get away.

As the body count rises, Kirstin finds she's a suspect, as well as a potential victim. If the killer isn't caught soon, someone might well be writing Kirstin's obituary...

ALSO AVAILABLE

Reap What You Sow - Bloodhound Books

Struggling journalist Sophie can't believe her luck when she lands the job of a lifetime—writing the personal history of renowned geneticist Tim Henderson, from his idyllic Greek island. But the island, and Henderson, turn out to be hiding much more than Sophie bargained for.

5 stars
"A compelling psychological thriller that is always one step ahead of the reader, a great read." (Amazon Review.)

"Totally gripping. I loved this book. Couldn't put it down and read it more or less in one sitting." (Amazon Review.)

BOOK TWO - A SALE OF PROMISES

'Sadly, Florida didn't suit me.' Julia said, stirring her iced macchiato with the end of a straw.

'Oh,' Carris replied, a look of concern scudding over the library assistant's thin, pinched features. 'Why was that?'

Julia wasn't really sure she wanted to go into great detail on this. The small Suffolk village where she had initially lived for thirty years had not been entirely truthful with her. Therefore, she wondered if she was duty-bound to reply with any kind of honesty whatsoever. She had, after all, made her grand exit and hadn't wanted to return quite so quickly. Or indeed, at all. But fate often had other plans, and it clearly hadn't finished its fun with Julia. True, it had been twelve months since her final retirement speech in the function room above the Dog and Duck, and she had not returned to the actual village, refusing to set foot within a ten-mile radius of the place. However, even returning to the county itself could not help but strike the proud ex-library manager as a backward step.

'Was it the crocodiles?' Carris asked.

'No. They have alligators.' Julia corrected.

'So, was it the alligators?'

'Not really.' Julia said, toying with her straw, 'I mean, I can't say that I liked them, but I avoided swimming in swamps.'

Carris nodded as if to say this was all very sensible. 'Was it the poisonous snakes?'

Julia shook her head. 'I always wore long trousers and something more substantial than flip-flops when trekking through long grasses. There are very few boa constrictors in the Everglades. So, with sensible shoes and long chinos, the snakes don't present problems.'

Suddenly, Carris beamed with excitement. 'Of course—baseball caps!'

Julia ran her fingers gently through her grey curling hair—hair that she had always been proud of. 'I certainly didn't like the way they squash everything down,' she admitted. 'But they're not compulsory.'

'Oh?' Carris looked surprised. 'I didn't realise.'

Julia nodded. 'Many people don't.'

'Oh, Julia, please. What made you come back?' Carris flopped her head on the table in front of her as if she were a child wanting a biscuit. A number of people in the small post office café looked around. They didn't know Carris. She was miles from home. So, they most likely would have thought the thin, wiry woman was a bit odd which, of course, was exactly what she was.

'Julia!' Carris implored. 'Did you miss us?'

'Of course I missed you.' The older woman said. She had been a little hurt when she had understood the true extent of the village cover-up—the one which had gone on so merrily without her. She had felt betrayed since she had been in the frame for the actual murder. But she had soon been cleared, and on reflection, despite the false imprisonment, the village cover-up of murder, and the lies, none of that had stopped her from missing the people she had left behind. People that she had lived alongside in that small, rural village for over thirty years.

'It was the healthcare,' Julia confessed, putting poor Carris out of her misery. 'That's why I left Florida.'

'Ahhh.' Carris exhaled in satisfied delight as if she had finally been given the keys to the kingdom.

'I can't begin to tell you how much I had to pay when I got an ingrown toenail.' Julia said, still a little upset about the atrocity of the bill.

Carris' screwed her face into an attitude of sympathy. 'That's what flip-flops do. Too much freedom for the toes.'

Julia wasn't sure this was strictly true, but somewhere in Florida, she discovered she had lost the will to argue, correct or instruct. Besides, other things needed discussion.

'And Des?' Julia asked gently. 'What happened there?' Des was the wonderful, apologetic and slightly simple postman that Carris had fallen so head over heels for only twelve months previously. It had seemed like a union crafted in heaven.

'Oh,' Carris exhaled with all the finesse of a deflating balloon. 'I didn't suit Des.'

'Ah,' Julia replied, knowing that in matters of the heart, it was wise not to push or question and that when a long-standing friend gives you this particular kind of information, there was only one form of reply that will do. Therefore, Julia quickly put it into place. 'The man's a fool.'

Carris nodded sadly, clearly hiding a deep well of pain and hurt, and Julia found herself wishing that she had been there. That she had not been off and about, gallivanting around Florida, avoiding alligators and poisonous snakes—

that she had been around to wipe Carris' tears and give the poor woman a hug.

As if having direct access to Julia's thoughts, Carris reached across the table and squeezed the ex-librarian's hand.

'I'm glad that you're back.'

In truth, Julia had been back for eight months. The ingrown toenail incident had happened soon after arriving in the US, and it had not taken long for Julia to realise that this large country of heat, strange animals and odd things called grits was not for a woman in her autumn years. Not unless that woman happened to have the backing of a sitcom franchise, since Julia's savings appeared to burn through quicker than a Californian wildfire.

Julia had flirted briefly with the possibility of returning to Wales but decided she had been out of the game for too long. Besides, Suffolk had suited her. Fortunately, she had remained in contact with Reece, the solicitor who had attempted once to betray Julia and now felt eternally (and useful) in her debt. It was Reece who had told her about the small village of Hoxne, in an Area of Outstanding Natural Beauty with a lot of history, no library, a pub, a post office and a cast of colourful locals who prided themselves on keeping their noses out of other people's business. Since it was on the Norfolk border, nobody would recognise her there. She could live out her days peacefully in the quaint but tiny holiday cottage owned by Reece. Taking her ingrown toenail to the Accident and Emergency department in Ipswich for only the price of a bus fair, which was cheap since Julia had spent her life paying her taxes and was over sixty, it had felt like a no-brainer.

'Why didn't you come back to our village?' Carris asked, looking dismissively around the dusty shop, with its beams of trapped light and cobwebs. 'You could have lived with me.'

Julia shook her head. 'After what happened…'

'I know. I know.' Carris reached out her other hand. 'But still.'

In fact, Julia had not even told Carris where she was living. It had only been this morning, as Julia walked to the post office to pick up a ball of string, that she had seen the library vehicle thundering down the hill with Carris at the wheel.

'How long have you been driving the library van?' Julia asked, curious as to the circumstances of her own precious library.

'Around a month.' Carris said, finding herself full of a sudden, gushing joy. 'Just imagine if I hadn't started driving. I would never have known you were back.'

'No,' said Julia, aware that this was a bitter-sweet experience.

'I couldn't go on in the library without you, Julia. I've always loved driving a van. So…' the recently mobile librarian said brightly. 'It seemed like a good fit.'

'Yes,' Julia replied thoughtfully.

'And you, Julia?' Carris asked, rushing to try to get all the facts. To pin Julia into place just as you might pin down a butterfly. 'Why settle here?' Carris' cheeks pinched together as though she was sucking something very sour and not too pleasant as she ran her eyes once again around the small medieval coffee shop with a damp smell of cut wood, elderly people bent over their coffee and newspapers and that stale smell.

Julia could see that it didn't have the same vitality as Carris' home village.

'I mean,' Carris said with a sneer, 'sneeze, and you'll be

in Norfolk. What do you do in a place like this?' She glanced down at the dark wooden table with its drinks menu and events flyer.

'An auction of promises,' Carris read. 'What even is that?'

'People sell off favours. It's coming up next month.'

'Will there be a disco?' Carris asked.

'I think that's unlikely. You'd have to look at the sales catalogue.'

Carris laughed. Julia had no idea why. Possibly, it was nerves or a lack of understanding as to what a sales catalogue actually was, even though this was blatantly obvious on account of the name.

'There's a lot going on here.'

Carris gave her friend a disbelieving gaze.

'Enough,' Julia conceded. 'And there's an awful lot of history.'

Carris raised a disbelieving eyebrow. She had never been one for history.

'I'm currently working for an academic,' Julia continued, enjoying the sound of her own words—words which were surely well suited to an ex-librarian. 'A historian. I'm doing some organisation for him on St Edmund, who was killed just down the road.'

Carris looked shocked.

'A long time ago, 900 AD. It's all water under the bridge now. In fact, he was killed under the bridge. Long story,' Julia sighed. 'But it keeps me busy.'

Carris yawned.

'And there's more. One of the largest finds of treasure. It was discovered in these very fields.' Julia waved one arm towards the back of the store, which opened out onto a bucolic setting of open pastures. 'The place is steeped in history, myths, legends…'

Yes,' Carris said, not a whole heap interested, 'but do you have a decent chip van?'

At the mention of a chip van, Julia felt her shoulders rising. She still remembered all too well the distribution of poisonous plants to an entire village in order to cover the tracks of a murder. Much of this distribution was handled by Captain Crispy and his van during his Thursday fry ups.

'I just think you might find this place a little…' Carris sniffed, 'dull. There's not enough happening.'

Julia had, in fact, grown to love dull. 'I'm sure I shall be fine. What days do you come through in your van, Carris?'

Carris flipped open her notebook and looked through her schedule. 'Wednesdays around one-ish.'

'Fabulous,' Julia said, making a mental note never to walk through the village for a ball of string on a Wednesday ever again.

'It's been so wonderful to see you,' Carris called from the window of her large, colourful van. 'But seriously, Julia, I mean this place,' she glanced around at the tumbleweed street, with the houses clustered sleepily around a thin triangle of green. 'It is so boring. You really should come home. There's never a dull moment.'

Julia had decided in Florida that dull moments were exactly what she wanted now. Therefore, "home" would most definitely not be the right place. But she simply smiled and replied. 'I'll certainly think about it.'

Carris waved as she pulled away, leaving a small puff of diesel smoke in her wake, and Julia turned from the café. Standing for a moment in a shaft of golden winter sunshine. Yes, this was peace. This was tranquillity. This was…

'Murder!' Somebody shouted. Julia squinted behind her towards the path leading down from the woods, and her heart caught in her chest. There was a woman running frantic, distraught and shoeless down the hill towards Julia.

'Murder,' the woman gasped. Her terrified eyes burned into Julia's soul. 'Please help me. Please help.'

ACKNOWLEDGMENTS

With thanks also to James Holloway and Emma Struthers, for helping me develop the character of Julia many moons ago as a one-woman show. Thanks also to Adrianne (who played that one woman) and to Sian Woods for her lovely voice coaching. Yet more thanks to Richard Waites, who bounced around ideas with me for a TV sitcom set in a rural library.

With special thanks to BetaBreck, who helped me with their expert BetaRead. To Isla who gave the project the once over. To Megan Cook for her line reading and proofreading and Sophie Taylor for her final proofread and comments.

It takes a village!

SIGN UP FOR THE NEWSLETTER

The newsletter comes out once a month. I'll be reviewing what to watch and read. Unsubscribe anytime.